THE COMPLETE CASES
OF CORPUS DELICTI MORT

THE COMPLETE CASES OF

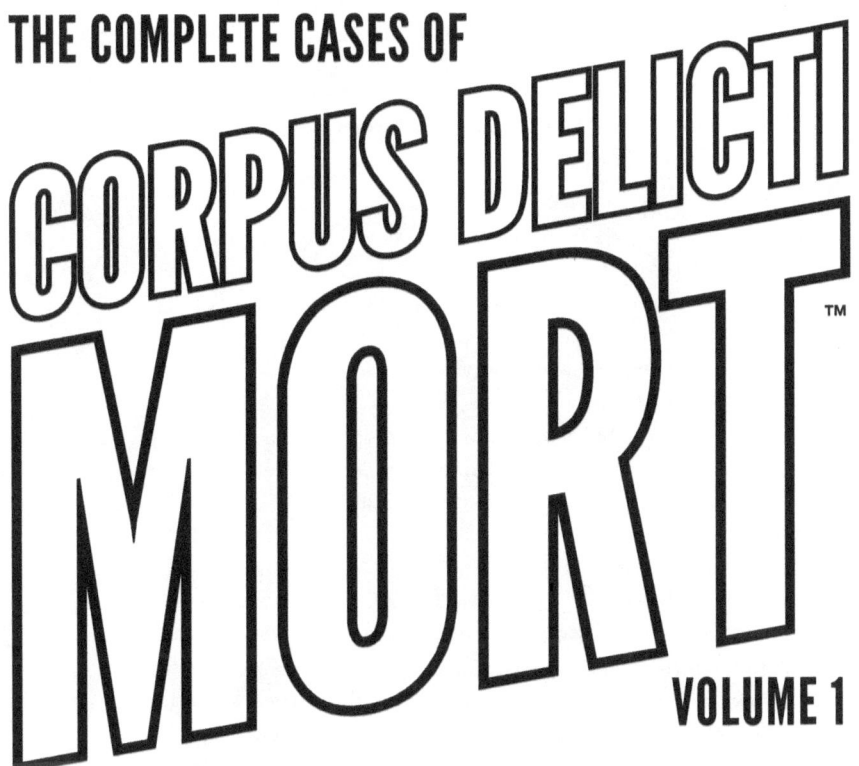

CORPUS DELICTI MORT™

VOLUME 1

JULIUS LONG

ILLUSTRATIONS BY
JOSEPH SZOKOLI
RAFAEL DESOTO

POPULAR PUBLICATIONS • 2021

TABLE OF CONTENTS

C.D. FOR CORPUS DELICTI

"WE ARRANGE THIS PHONY MURDER, SEE," EXPLAINED LUCKY PAGE. "THEN WE TELL BERRY THAT HER PLAYBOY BROTHER IS IN A JAM AND NEEDS REAL LEGAL HELP—$100,000 WORTH. AND THAT MEANS YOU! YOUR CUT WILL BE HALF. ARE YOU INTERESTED?" CLARENCE DARROW MORT WAS ALWAYS INTERESTED IN A HUNDRED GRAND, OR ANY PORTION THEREOF. HE DIDN'T KNOW THEN THAT REAL MURDER WOULD STEP UNANNOUNCED INTO THE SCHEME OR THAT HE'D BE FIGHTING DESPERATELY FOR THE LIFE OF THE VERY GUY HE'D HOPED TO PLAY FOR A SUCKER.

C LARENCE DARROW MORT realized that he had grown to love his fellow men. He knew that he was drunk and that it was time he was home in bed.

He slid off his bar stool and walked a little too erectly toward the checkroom. This was on the opposite side of the Riviera Club, and Mort had only approached his destination when Phil Sinton, the club manager, blocked his path.

"The boss wants to see you, Mr. Mort."

Mort replied with dignity: "But I don't want to see your boss. Tell Lucky to go to hell."

Sinton did not change expression. He said quietly: "It has to be now, Mr. Mort. Just come with me."

Customers were staring. But the extreme courtesy that gloved Sinton's firm command enabled Mort to comply without losing face. He knew that he had best comply. Lucky Page was absolute master of the Riviera—every waiter doubled in muscle. Mort followed Sinton through the crowded night club.

He was led into the room which was Page's real source of revenue. Page boasted that there was a million dollars' worth of gambling equipment here, and anyone who saw the layout felt inclined to agree. At the far end of the gambling room was a plain walnut door which Sinton opened without knocking. He did knock at a second door a few yards beyond. There was a grunt from within, and both men entered.

Lucky Page sat at a massive carved desk. He nodded to Sinton, who quickly stepped outside. Mort subsided a little unsteadily into a billowy leather chair. Page smiled engagingly.

"Nice victory you won today, C.D. I doubt if Darrow himself could have got that guy off, even if he was alive."

He noticed the look on Mort's face and said: "Oh, I forgot, C.D., how you don't like anyone reminding you that you were named after Darrow. My mistake. No offense meant."

"That," said Mort coldly, "is an understatement. I not only dislike any allusion to the derivation of my given and middle names, but I am inclined to make something of it. If you were not a big, powerful ox, and I were not almost helplessly drunk, I should knock your teeth down your throat."

Lucky Page chuckled. "For the life of me, I don't know why you take it that way. Clarence Darrow was the greatest criminal lawyer of his day. It's an honor to be named after him."

Mort managed an alcoholic shrug. "True, Darrow possessed that high degree of animal cunning that passes for a great legal mind. Outside the courtroom he even betrayed intelligence of an enviable degree. I admired and respected him a great deal, still do. But I can never forgive my father for naming me after him."

Page looked baffled. "But, C.D., you've been doing all right. Your father gave you a break. You must have made twenty grand getting that guy off today."

A forlorn smile passed across Mort's face. "Again my namesake has plagued me. Darrow defended many a penniless man—today I labored for the same reward. Lately my clients have been almost exclusively indigents. I trust that this explains why the check I cashed here last week was worthless. However, my luck is bound to change. A wealthy murderer will sooner or later come along. So if you will just give me a reasonable time, say thirty days..."

Page roared with laughter.

"So you thought I had you brought in here about a check? Didn't even know you'd cashed one here, C.D. I'll tell Phil it's all right. He looks after all the bookkeeping."

MORT FELT somewhat relieved, though it irked him to be under any obligation to Page. He remembered the days when the gambler had operated a

Berry Bangs suppressed a scream. "Good heavens! There *is* a body! The girl *is* dead!" she gasped.

shady roadhouse with slot machines strategically located where drunks couldn't miss them. Page had not been above strong-arming any drunk so incredibly lucky as to hit a jackpot.

"If it's not the check, Page, what's on your mind?"

"One hundred thousand dollars. Your cut will be half of it. Are you interested?"

"I am always interested in one hundred thousand dollars or any portion thereof."

Page laughed his satisfaction. He laughed from the bottom of his belly, but the laugh fell short of heartiness. Mort felt uncomfortable.

"Get to the point, Page."

"This is it: You know Jetur Bangs, don't you? Well, the kid's on my cuff for a hundred grand. That's a lot of dough for a guy like me to lose."

"It's a lot of dough," Mort commented coolly, "but you haven't lost it. What you really mean is that your gimmicks out there short-changed the sucker for that many markers. And now that his old man has died and left his inheritance tied up in a spendthrift trust, you're hooked."

Page eyed Mort with resentment, but he managed a smile.

"I never knew how to take you, C.D. But I'm cutting you in anyway. We're going to collect that hundred grand."

"You may omit the 'we.' I'm out. I don't care for a wild goose chase when the money is on a contingent basis. In the first place, your gambling debt has no legal standing—you couldn't sue and collect a dime even if Jetur had the money. In the second place, there's no chance that he will have. His sister, Berry Bangs, is trustee of the spendthrift trust, and she would laugh in our faces if we asked her to pay off. If you're thinking about breaking the will, that's out, too. The fact that Old Man Bangs tied up Jetur's money is ample evidence that he possessed all his marbles. He well knew that if the moron got the dough in his own hands he'd give it away to chiselers like you."

Page writhed at the insult, but like a good disciple of Machiavelli or Dale Carnegie, he came up smiling.

"Sure, C.D., I know the deal's against me, but I still got an angle. In my book it can't miss. Suppose Jetur gets himself into a jam, a bad jam. What would his sister, Berry, do in a case like that? She'd have to front for him, of course! She's strictly Social with a capital S. She couldn't stand having her brother do time or fry."

Mort sat back interestedly in his chair.

"Go on."

"I thought you'd like the idea, C.D. Here's the layout as I've planned it: You know Sonia Renoir, my blues singer. She's been driving Jetur just about nuts. Couple of weeks ago he gave her an engagement ring with a three-carat rock in it. Only she wouldn't take Jetur along with it. So the chump lets her keep it, and she's wearing it now on her right hand.

"Sure, it's a laugh. Sonia'd have taken Jetur quickly enough only she knows how his dough's tied up. So here's how we use the situation—tonight I send Sonia home early. Jetur follows her to her apartment at the Sherry Arms. He goes in the front way right past the desk clerk, though he rates a special key to the back door. It's Sonia's way of kidding the boys. She gives them a pass to first base, but when they get there they find out how far it is to home plate.

"Jetur comes downstairs after being up there only a few minutes. Then he goes to the family mansion, wakes up his sister and tells her a hell of a story. He's just walked in on

Sonia and found her stretched out all dead with her head smashed to jelly. The ring he's given her is gone. He's afraid it'll look as if they had a row over the ring and he lost his head and killed her.

"So that means Jetur needs legal help—real legal help. And that means you! You're the only mouthpiece in town that people think of when they're in real murder trouble. And you're the only guy who could get away with telling Berry it'll cost a hundred grand of her brother's money to get him off. Get it?"

"I could hardly miss it," Mort replied coldly. "Disbarment, I mean. As soon as Berry's sister tumbled to the fraud, she'd have me hanged from the highest limb. No thanks, I want no part of that deal for a lousy fifty-fifty cut of a hundred grand!"

"But you haven't let me finish. Berry Bangs will never get wise. It's like this: Sonia's set to take a powder. She's hooked a West Coast millionaire who's going to take her away from all this. She'll drop out of show business, and nobody around here will ever see her pretty face again. There'll be no tell-tale publicity about her wedding on the Coast, because she'll be married under her real name, Mabel McNabb. She'll cooperate on account of I introduced her to her millionaire."

Mort regarded Page. "So Sonia's taking a trip! Well, I'll give her credit for keeping it quiet."

"Sure, she's played it down, all right. A smart girl, Sonia. Well, can I count you in?"

Mort nodded slowly. "I'm in. But how about Jetur? Will he go for it?"

Page chuckled. "He knows better than to refuse!" He pressed a button. The door opened, and Phil Sinton appeared. "Bring in Jetur."

SINTON VANISHED and presently reappeared with a too-handsome youth slightly the worse for liquor. He nodded casually to Mort.

"Mr. Mort's agreed to our proposition," Page announced. "We're going to put it over tonight."

Jetur Bangs frowned. "I've been thinking. If I've got to go through with this lousy swindle to pay you dough you rooked me out of in the first place, I want something out of it besides the ride."

Page frowned unpleasantly. "Meaning what?"

"Meaning we may as well raise the ante to a hundred and fifty grand and cut it three ways. Then I'll get mine. After all, it's my own money!"

"You'll get yours," Page told him, "if you try to throw a monkey wrench into this deal. It's bad enough my losing fifty grand on you. Don't make me think about how bad I feel. Besides, even Mort couldn't raise the ante for the job. It'll be the same price!"

Jetur managed to twist defiance into his handsome features.

"I still say it's fifty grand for me or no dice!"

Phil Sinton had been waiting for Page's eye. He got it, stepped quickly behind Jetur and did something to Jetur's arm that Mort couldn't see. Jetur screamed.

"For God's sake, let go!" He was the color of a sheet. Sinton made no effort to relax his grip.

Page spoke with sarcasm.

"Is it still no dice?"

"Damn it, make him let me go. I was just kiddin'!"

Sinton stepped back. Jetur seemed on the verge of tears as he rubbed his arm. Slowly, color returned to his face. Page chuckled amusedly.

"Sure you've got your lines right, Jetur?" he asked menacingly.

"Yeah."

Mort had watched the goings-on with growing nausea.

"I don't like this deal. Suppose the boy's sister wants proof of a corpus delicti. What then?"

"Oh, I expected her to check with the desk man at the Sherry. That's why Jetur's going to show up, just in case. That'll give her all the scare she'll need. She'll pay quickly enough."

Mort shook his head. "I still don't like it. But I'll go along."

"If anything goes wrong," Page said sourly, "it'll be your fault. Sure you're sober enough to handle it?"

Mort rose stiffly, not deigning to reply. He strode back into the night club. Page had been unable to guess how completely sobering the interview had been. So Sonia was eloping with a West Coast millionaire!

He paused, for she was in the middle of a number.

She had about as much voice as a strip teaser, and though she would have been outraged at the comparison, she got by for the same reason. Her body was perfect. Her hair was black and straight and fell to the waist of her backless gown. Women sneered at that straight hair, but men stared with strange intensity.

Sonia sang to a white-thatched customer at a front table. As Mort watched, Page appeared and joined the man. He would be the West Coast find, of course. There was a diamond ring on a finger of each of Sonia's hands now. Though the one on the right hand was at times blinding, the new one moved about in the spotlight with the startling effect of a comet.

Mort got his hat and left the night club. Outside, the doorman signaled for a cab, but he waved a hand.

"It's a nice night. I'll walk."

He had walked only a few steps when a black sedan drew up beside him and halted. He turned, then froze in his tracks.

AT PRECISELY two forty-five his apartment phone rang. He permitted it to ring four times, then answered.

"I must see you, Mr. Mort!" It was a feminine voice. "It's a matter of life and death!"

"Who is speaking?"

"Bernice Bangs. I must see you at once." Mort permitted a few seconds to pass before answering. The nocturnal caller, of course, was the Berry Bangs of the rotogravure and society pages, but only members of her inner circle of select friends would have dared use her nickname.

"Your business can't be so important, Miss Bangs, that it can't wait till morning. Supposing you drop into my office at, let's say ten."

"This can't wait until morning. I'm coming right over."

She hung up. Mort smiled enigmatically as he cradled the phone. Fifteen minutes later his bell rang. He opened the door. Berry Bangs and Jetur walked into his room without ceremony.

"So sorry to get you up, Mr. Mort," Berry said carelessly, "but my brother's in a jam. Have you got a cigarette? I'm fresh out and so's Jetur."

Mort ushered the pair into his library and provided cigarettes. Jetur avoided his eyes completely.

Berry took a quick drag on her cigarette and said: "Jetur's been playing with a canary named Sonia something-or-other at the Riviera. Got a voice like nothing but plenty of figure." As if to illustrate, Berry loosed a cape, exposing a strapless evening gown. Red-gold hair touched her beautifully molded shoulders. Mort compared Sonia Renoir and unfavorably.

"I've heard the lady sing," he admitted.

"Sure, all the wolves in town have. She's played everything in pants. So what does Jetur here do but pay a call on her tonight after she quits at the Riviera. He walks right in on her and finds her flat on the floor with her brains soaking into the rug. Then he brightly beats it out the front way, the same way he came in. The desk man at the Sherry saw him make both trips, so that means Jetur'll be the top man in the pinch parade as soon as the body's discovered. So I decided he needed real legal talent. In this town that means you."

Mort bowed slightly. "I am indeed honored. However, I'm not sure that I care to take this case. Juries are inclined to be prejudiced against wealthy young playboys such as Jetur. I'm afraid—"

"Nonsense!" said Berry. "You've handled tougher cases than this, and Jetur may even be innocent, as he says. If it's fees you're worried about, name your own price!"

Mort reflected, shook his head as if against his better judgment.

"One hundred thousand dollars," he said quietly.

Berry started. "Why, that's—" She caught herself, muttered, "I guess I asked for it," and took a checkbook from her handbag. She hastily scribbled a check. Mort accepted it and thrust it casually into his left pocket.

"Very well, Miss Bangs, I shall handle your brother's case. I want him to go back to the Riviera and pretend that nothing at all has happened. It is imperative that he betray no consciousness of guilt. Of course, we will never admit that he found the girl murdered. His story must be that he left her alive and well."

Berry's brows drew together. "Not so fast, Mr. Mort. You can send Jetur to the Riviera all right, but as his trustee I'm going to have a look at the corpus delicti before I'm letting myself be accountable for an expenditure of a hundred thousand dollars. We're going, you and I, to the Sherry Arms."

Mort stiffened. "Miss Bangs, I am accustomed to conducting the defense of my clients according to my own methods. For us to go together to Sonia Renoir's apartment would be to point suspicion directly toward your brother. I certainly shall not go there!"

"Then you certainly shall not cash that check in the morning! You'll find that payment has been stopped!" Berry chuckled as she watched Mort with narrowed eyes. "Maybe I'm upsetting a little playhouse, huh? Listen, Mr. Mort, I'm an old hand at parrying Jetur's thrusts at his trust fund. He's used about every trick in the book to extract money from me, and maybe now he's trying a phony murder!"

Mort ventured a quick glance at Jetur and found him pale. He shrugged.

"Really, Miss Bangs, your tone is almost insulting. But since you insist, I see there is no alternative but to accede to your request, though—" He left off, shaking his head deprecatingly. Then he got his hat and accompanied the pair downstairs.

Jetur had driven his own car, and he went off to the Riviera. Mort climbed in beside Berry, who was driving a convertible of dimensions rivaling those of a Pullman car. She drove across town to the Sherry Arms, and Mort rode silently beside her.

The desk man at the Sherry smiled a greeting.

"Good evening, Mr. Mort! I suppose you—"

"We're calling on Miss Renoir," Mort cut him short. "She's expecting us, so we'll go right up."

This seemed to be all right with the desk man, though he looked a little wonderingly at Berry.

An automatic elevator carried them to the fourth floor. Mort led the girl without hesitation to a door. He pressed the bell button. There was no answer, and he pressed again. He tried the door, and it opened. He went inside, Berry at his heels.

She suppressed a scream. "Good heavens! There is a body! The girl is dead!"

BOTH STATEMENTS were correct. Sonia Renoir's body lay on her living room floor. She had been wearing a dressing gown, and apparently the struggle had all but torn it from her. The dark stain in the rug around the base of her skull left no doubt as to the result of the struggle. Her right hand lay across her body.

The diamond ring was missing.

Berry had apparently lost all desire to investigate the matter further.

"Let's get out of—" She stopped, stared, as a man appeared in the doorway.

"Hello, Joe," said Mort calmly. "Captain Wood, meet Miss Bangs. Joe's a homicide dick. Quick work, Joe. Somebody tip you?"

Wood nodded. "Yeah, C.D. Headquarters got a call there was a body in here, so I came out myself." He went over to the phone and sent for his crew. Then he came back and sat down. "What you doing here, C.D.?"

"I'm representing a client. Jetur Bangs. He walked in here and found this. So he got cold feet and ran out. So I'm surrendering him. He's at the Riviera."

Wood looked absently at the almost naked body on the floor. Sonia Renoir looked as if she might have fallen asleep there—unless you noticed the stain in the rug around her upturned head. Wood sighed regretfully, got up and stretched.

"Well, let's go and get Jetur. I got a patrolman on guard downstairs, so I'll send him up." He shook his head. "This is the worst jam Jetur's ever been in."

Berry was very pale as they rode downstairs. Wood gave curt instructions to the patrolman at the desk and to the man there, then the trio went outside. They used Wood's squad car.

The last show was under way when they arrived at the Riviera. Phil Sinton came up as they entered. He eyed Wood with alarm, Mort questioningly.

"Maybe we'd better have this out in Page's office," Mort suggested. Wood nodded. He watched as Mort crossed to the bar and halted beside Jetur perched on a bar stool.

"Come along, Jetur. We're going to the office for a little talk with a homicide dick." Apparently perplexed, Jetur slid off the stool. Mort said casually: "The girl's dead. Did you know that?"

He thought Jetur was going to faint. He caught his arm and steadied him.

"Easy does it. Now, keep your mouth shut about our deal. Let me do the talking!"

Deathly pale, Jetur walked beside him, Wood following. Phil Sinton had found Page, who came in, jocular and expansive.

"Help yourselves, folks! Always glad to accommodate an officer of the law. Would you folks like drinks served?" Nobody seemed interested. Page started to retire.

"Stick around," said Mort. "Since we're using your office, you may as well have a grandstand seat to the show. Besides, it was your singer who was murdered."

Page froze. "Murdered?" His eyes narrowed upon Mort's. "You, you—you're not kidding! Sonia really got herself murdered?"

Mort nodded. "We've just come from her apartment. Captain Wood wants to question Jetur."

Page stared at Jetur. So did Wood. "Come on, son. Let's hear your story."

Jetur told his story. If he had heard Mort's explicit instructions, he ignored them. He began from the beginning, telling in detail about his debt to Page, about the scheme to settle it by staging a phony murder. Like a cornered wildcat, he stared from Page to Mort.

"Damn it, I'm not going through with that yarn for anybody! Not when there's a murder rap to pin on me! Sonia was alive when I left her. I never touched her at all!"

Wood had listened delightedly. He grinned at Mort.

"How about it, C.D.? Is the kid telling the truth about the frame-up to shake loose a hundred grand?"

"Well, I—"

"Sure he is!" Page supplied. "Why try to conceal it? I wasn't doing anything wrong—just trying to get my money back. Now that it's really murder, I'm not covering up for anybody!"

Wood grinned gloatingly as Clarence Darrow Mort sat without a word to say.

"Looks as if you decided not to keep it a phony murder," he told Jetur. "Come on, son, let's have it. You couldn't stand seeing her go away with another guy, so you lost your head and let her have it. Right?"

Jetur shook his head stubbornly. "I was fed up with Sonia long ago. All I asked for was my ring back. She put up a squawk, but I got it, and she was alive enough when I left her."

WOOD'S EYES became sharp and alert.

"A ring? What ring?"

"A three-carat rock," Page supplied. "Jetur'd given it to her for an engagement ring, so she hung onto it even though she gave him the brush." He turned on Jetur. "So you decided you'd take the ring, huh? And she wouldn't give it back, so you had to conk her."

"I did not!" Jetur appealed to the detective. "Maybe you should ask Page a few things, too. He had ideas about Sonia himself!"

Wood smiled at Page. Page reddened.

"In case you got any ideas of dragging me into this deal, skip 'em. I've been right here all the time. I was sitting out at Mr. Caldwell's table, that's Sonia's boy-friend. Two hundred people saw me!"

Wood looked mildly bored. "If you had any dirty work to do, Lucky, you'd hardly do it yourself. What about Sinton?"

"He was right here all the time. Check on us both if you want to."

"Don't think I won't." Wood turned again to Jetur. "Let's see the ring, son."

Jetur produced a diamond ring. Wood regarded it, then dropped it into his pocket.

"Exhibit A," he explained. "Now tell me, son, what did you hit her with?"

"I tell you I didn't touch her! She was plenty mad about having to give back the ring, but she gave it back willingly enough when I threatened—" He stopped guiltily.

"Threatened what?"

"I told her I'd make a stink about her West Coast meal ticket. So she gave back the ring."

Wood said nothing. But his thought was clear. He sighed.

"Just a minute," said Berry Bangs. "Jetur wasn't the only boy-friend darling Sonia had. For example, the eminent counsel here!"

Wood regarded her interestedly.

"Go on."

"When we went to Sonia's apartment tonight, the desk man greeted Mr. Mort as if he were a frequent caller. Mort shut him up before he could give anything away, but later he gave himself away. He went directly to Sonia's floor without asking, and he knew where her apartment was when we got there. Maybe he's got one of her keys!"

Wood regarded Mort, who nodded.

"Sure, I have one of her keys. Why should I be an exception? I confess that I was quite fond of Sonia. I used to drop in at her place often. And, as my pal, Page, put it, I was visibly upset tonight when I learned that she was checking out. By the way, Page, thanks for the plug."

Page scowled. "I still think you're a good prospect for this murder, C.D. Even when you left I thought what a wonderful setup it was for anybody who wanted to rub out Sonia. And you looked as if you'd like to!"

Wood regarded Mort. "I hope you've got an alibi."

"I have. Page was kind enough to supply it for me. As I left here tonight, a squad car pulled up, and Hank Barnes, of the fraud squad, nailed me. Seems Page had signed an affidavit about a rubber check I left here last week. So I was an hour and a half rousing a magistrate and getting bail set. I'd just got home when Miss Bangs called. You can check with the fraud squad, Joe. It's a wonder you hadn't heard about it."

Wood eyed Page. "This true about that check?"

Page looked uncomfortable. "I'd have to check with Sinton." He seemed genuinely apologetic as he turned to Mort. "Sorry if it happened, C.D. Of course Sinton looks after all that stuff. He must have made a mistake in your case."

"Well, you can thank him for me. My alibi's perfect."

WOOD ADDRESSED Jetur. "I'm arresting you, son. The charge is murder. You'll really need a lawyer now."

"He has one," said Mort. "I've been retained and paid, and I'm defending him."

"The hell you are!" Berry Bangs shrieked fiercely. "I wouldn't let you defend my brother if you agreed to work for nothing! As for paying you—you just try to cash that check!"

Mort appealed to Jetur. "How about it? Do you want me to defend you, or don't you?"

"Well, I—"

"Suppose I could demonstrate to your satisfaction that I can win your case?"

"You—you think you can?"

"I'm morally certain. You see, I could give the jury an alternative theory as to who killed Sonia Renoir. I could show them that another person had a motive and an opportunity. For example, there is your sister, Berry. I learned tonight from the fraud squad that I'm not the only one so indiscreet as to hand out rubber checks. Only last week Berry herself was caught up on one."

Mort turned slowly in the dead silence and smiled at the girl.

"Of course you can imagine my surprise at learning that her bank account had deteriorated into such a precarious position. But Hank Barnes explained that in the last year the poor girl has taken an awful drubbing in the stock market and her inheritance is virtually exhausted.

"Does that astound you, Jetur, to know that your sister, who holds the purse strings on your spendthrift trust, has been even a greater spendthrift than you? Well, your own losses here at the Riviera are in a piker class compared to hers on the stock market. So even a jury could see that by framing you for murder and causing you to die in the electric chair she would inherit your trusteed fortune without strings!"

"This is ridiculous!" Berry Bangs blazed with contempt. "Of course the whole thing is fantastic!"

"I'll agree with that," said Wood. "Even if she had a motive for framing Jetur, how could she have known about the setup, the phony murder scheme?"

"From the victim herself. Jetur's told you how angry she was when he blackmailed her into giving up his ring. Her natural instinct would be to call Berry and give away the whole plot as revenge."

"You're getting better and better!" Berry scoffed. "How do you think I'd get into the slut's apartment? Even if I could get by the desk man without being seen!"

"You could have used the back entrance. As an old caller via the same route I know that the door was often carelessly left unlocked. As for getting into the apartment, Sonia would have been gratified at your call."

"You're an idiot! You know you're making up the whole thing out of whole cloth! You can't prove a thing!"

Mort shrugged. "My dear Miss Bangs, I have no desire to do so. I am not at all concerned with turning in the culprit guilty of Sonia Renoir's murder. I am only interested in raising a reasonable doubt in the minds of the jury which tries your brother. I'll leave it to Joe Wood as to whether my little theory would accomplish that purpose."

Wood eyed Berry gravely. "Unless you've got an alibi—"

"Of course I have! Jetur himself knows I was at home when he got there!"

"You still could have done it," said Jetur sullenly. "I stopped for a couple of drinks on the way from Sonia's."

"Jetur! You don't think for a minute that—"

"The hell I don't!" Jetur crossed and looked her in the eye. "I wouldn't put anything past you, my darling little sister! Do you think I don't know you tricked Dad into putting that spendthrift trust into his will?"

He turned his back on Berry as he faced Mort.

"I'm hiring you, Mr. Mort. I think you've got the right slant as to who killed Sonia. And maybe it'll be a good idea to check up on the way she's been handling that trust fund of mine. If I know Berry—"

Wood shouted, and Jetur never finished. Berry had doubled her knee and snatched off a slipper. Its narrow heel was directed toward the back of Jetur's head in a vicious arc when Wood leaped forward and caught her arm. She dug his face with her nails. He snapped bracelets upon her wrists.

"So that's the way you did it, with the heel of your shoe! We'll have to take a look for a bloody heel in your wardrobe. Or would you like to confess right now?"

She called him a vile name. Mort shook his head deprecatingly.

"As Hank Barnes said about the rubber check, it happens in the best of families."

NO MINIMUM FOR MURDER

THERE IS NO MOTIVE POWERFUL ENOUGH TO MAKE SOME MEN KILL. FOR OTHERS, THE SLIGHTEST, PETTIEST PROVOCATION WILL SUFFICE—A WRONG WORD, A CARELESS GESTURE OR ONE MILLION DOLLARS.

CLARENCE DARROW MORT, the famous criminal lawyer, and four other lawyers were seated around a back table at Milligan's saloon. The subject under discussion was murder. Mort held the floor by common consent, for he had that day secured the acquittal of his hundredth client, a garage mechanic accused of liquidating his wife with a Stillson wrench, a tire iron and a cold chisel.

"The verdict was just," said Mort.

"You can't be serious," said Walter Price, a corporation lawyer. "Sam Anderson had an airtight case against that mechanic. I don't see how he missed. Evidently he's not the district attorney I thought he was."

"Don't blame Sam. He failed to get a conviction for a damn good reason. He couldn't prove motive. That mechanic had always got along with his wife—there simply wasn't any reason shown for him to kill her."

"Oh, he did it, all right," commented Harry Sylvester, a young and rising criminal lawyer. "Why else would he have taken those garage tools home with him that particular night?"

Mort shrugged. "On the other hand, why should he have taken them home to kill his wife? What was his motive in killing her?"

"Why didn't the judge throw out the case if the D.A. didn't prove any motive?" It was a new voice, that of Ned Dumont, whose practice was limited to divorce cases. Mort eyed him as if he were a backward child.

"Ned, it's plain to see that you've let your criminal law grow rusty. If I had moved for a dismissal on the ground that no motive was shown, Sam Anderson would have made a fool out of me by citing the case of Liggins vs. U.S., 297 Federal, page 881. The case is fresh in my mind because I doublechecked the motive angle. It holds that proof of motive is not an essential element of homicide."

Ned Dumont reddened. Mort quickly attempted to pour balm on his wounded vanity. "I doubt if anybody here but Harry had the right slant on motive. Anyway, you were really right in lending it that much importance. Though a conviction for murder can be legally obtained without a showing of the motive, it is practically impossible to get a jury to convict unless motive is proved."

"And you've got to come up with a strong motive," added Harry Sylvester, "not just a petty, insignificant one."

Mort nodded. "Many a murderer has gone scot-free because a jury was incapable of appreciating that any human being could commit such a vile deed upon such a trivial motive. Just as there is no motive powerful enough to make some men kill, others need only the slightest, pettiest provocation. When it comes to motive for murder, there is no minimum requirement."

"**I WISH** you would tell me," said a thick voice from the far side of the table, "just what the hell you are talking about."

The shot roared deafeningly, Phil Sinton
had drawn and fired so fast that by the time
Carter had seen him it was too late.

It was Al Carter. These days Carter rarely drew a sober breath. He had a complete lack of ambition and a rich wife, and he had acquired them in the order named.

Mort looked across the table and smiled indulgently.

"Sure, Al. What I mean is that a jury is inclined to misjudge human behavior. It is pathetically optimistic. It simply refuses to believe in the inherent pettiness of the human race. Never try to tell it that a man would commit murder for a few dollars. A few hundreds of dollars maybe, and thousands, yes. Perhaps the jurors are judging the accused by themselves."

"Perhaps," said Sylvester, "they dare not commit themselves. To admit that others could kill for a paltry prize would be to admit that they can understand such an act."

Mort nodded approvingly. "I see that I have one under-standing listener. You can appreciate my point when I say that there is absolutely no minimum motive for the committing of a murder even in second degree. To illus-trate, I one time freed a lady accused of having shot her husband. This time, too, no motive was shown. When we had left the courtroom and got back to my office, I said: 'Of course it's none of my business, but I have a certain profes-sional curiosity which I hope you will pardon. Whatever made you kill that man?'

"She wouldn't tell me then, but months afterwards she did. 'I killed him,' she said, 'because of the way he ate corn on the cob. He got it all over his fingers, and he would end up with butter clear to his ears. I stood it for fifteen years, then I could stand it no longer.'"

From the far side of the table came a grunt. "I still wish you would tell me what you're talking about!"

There was quiet laughter in which Mort did not share. He eyed Carter coldly.

"You're a sight, Al. I'm a firm believer in a man's right to ruin himself, but you're abusing the privilege."

Carter stared with glazed eyes. He hiccuped.

"Listen to who's talking! The one and only Clarence Darrow Mort! The guy who can go on a month's bender with a dozen clients in the klink! And you're telling me I'm drinking too much!"

Mort became pale. This was a sure sign that his temper had flared almost beyond control. But he did master it this time. He rose abruptly from the table and strode from the saloon.

There was a round of silence at the back table, then Harry Sylvester ordered a round of beers. Carter sipped his own, then looked around pleadingly.

"You don't blame me, do you, for sounding off? Hell, he may be a hot-shot criminal lawyer, but he's a souse just the same. Isn't that right, fellows?"

"Sure," replied Sylvester. "That's right, but that's not what got his goat. He couldn't stand your calling him Clarence Darrow Mort. Remind him he was named after Darrow, and he'll be your enemy for life."

"It does seem," conceded Carter, "that I did hear of that. It was his father, wasn't it, who named him after Darrow?"

"It was. And Mort is convinced that it was that circumstance that ruined his life. If he hadn't been named after Darrow, he says, he never would have been hoodwinked into a profession which he loathes. The name determined his destiny."

"Well, what's he got to beef about? Isn't he the tops? He's even been written up in *Time-Week*. Most of the lawyers I know would give their right arms to be in his shoes!"

"So would Mort," said Walter Price. "I mean he would give his right arm rather than step out of his own shoes. He can't fool me. The way he acts about being a lawyer is just an act. If he's soured on the profession, why does he have the biggest law library in town?"

The others exchanged thoughtful glances.

"You may have something there," conceded Sylvester. "Come to think about it, he's the only lawyer in town who has every series of the *National Reporter System*. Most of us think we're flying if we keep up with the *Northeastern*. Old Judge Crawford once got drunk and let a salesman sell him the *Atlantics*, but none of us at this table would think of such extravagance."

Price nodded. "And he cuts the books, too. Ask any judge. The reason he gets away with so much is that the judges are afraid he may be right." He lowered his voice.

"Besides that, I don't think he really drinks as much as he pretends."

At this there was an uproar of protest.

"It's all right maybe to talk about C.D. a little behind his back," said Sylvester, "but that's going too far!"

THE TAXICAB that picked up C.D. Mort outside Milligan's moved at his request to the south and night-club infested side of town. Mort had designated the Lucky Club, owned by Lucky Page, whom Mort cordially despised. Page, however, possessed one virtue which Mort could at this moment appreciate. Page would honor his checks.

Mort was stony broke. He did not have cab fare. He did not have change for a quarter. His colleagues back at Milligan's would have been astounded if they had been told that his sudden exit had been prompted by expedience rather than indignation. He had chosen to make an incident of Al Carter's drunken remark for the practical reason that he could not stand a round of drinks, and it was his turn next.

Mort made money. His fees were not so fabulous as rumored, but they were more than sufficient to support a first-class spendthrift. Mort was no spendthrift. He was merely a man through whose fingers money flowed like water. Every time he would pocket a sizable fee he would tell himself that this time he would salt it away. His resolve would endure perhaps three weeks, then the bank would send him a polite note, and he would be confounded.

His financial problems were complicated by his propensity to take on charity cases at a time when bills were due. The mere maintenance of his law library cost him thousands, and he would spend unstintingly upon detectives and expert testimony for a client who would never pay a fee. The garage mechanic he had that day freed was a case in point. The nominal retainer had long since been spent, and there would be no more.

Mort leaned back in the cab and felt sorry for himself. This last trial had taken only four days, but, as always at the end of a murder case, his nerves were exhausted. There was nothing he could do about it. He knew that by midnight he would consume a dozen doubles, but the liquor would not even give him a lift. Even benzedrine sulphate tablets would not help—they would only keep him awake all night.

But he was going to tank up anyway. Lucky Page could be counted on to cash his check, for Lucky had once, through a clerical oversight, caused his arrest in the matter of an old one. Since then Lucky had been outdoing himself to prove his good will. He had almost begged Mort to cash another check, not a good one, but one that was sure to bounce.

Mort was about to gratify his whim.

The cab deposited him in front of the Lucky Club, and he took the driver inside with him by express invitation, for he was not a man to bring out the cynicism in others.

"Well!" said Lucky Page. "Look who's here! Congratulations on getting that guy off today! Nobody but you could have done it!"

"Thanks," said Mort. "I would like to cash a check."

Lucky beamed. "Come right into my office."

"I'll be delighted."

Mort left the cab driver, slightly impressed now by the warmth of Lucky's welcome of his fare. All the way to Lucky's office Mort had been trying to make up his mind how much to stick him. To give a rubber check for only thirty or forty dollars would be in awkward taste. It was a situation which he could in decency place no man, even a heel like Lucky. A sensible sum would be one hundred dollars. But then Lucky's overtures had left the door open even wider. By the time Mort reached the office he had settled on two-fifty.

"You've been quite a stranger," said Lucky. He was a fat man in the night club tradition, a little bald to boot. He got out a blank check, and Mort filled it in. He handed it over to Lucky without daring to look at him.

Lucky seemed in ecstasy as he opened his safe. He took out a tiny packet of bills held together by a paper clip. He tossed them to the desk at which Mort sat.

"There's five bills there. Your check was for only half that, but you can pay me back when you feel like it. Maybe you'll want to get your feet wet at the tables."

"Thanks, but I'm keeping them dry," replied Mort. He had no objection to owing Lucky two-fifty or even five hundred, but he did not care to owe him twenty or thirty thousand. It was rumored that the man who had wired Lucky's tables had formerly held the chair for higher electrical engineering at a famous university and that his fee had been a percentage of the first year's take. He had, as a consequence, been able to retire from his chair to spend the remainder of his days in a thirty-room bungalow with as many baths, a swimming pool and four tennis courts.

Lucky remained on, for he was a man of ambitions. Mort sensed that Lucky desired to cultivate him, for in his racket he never knew when he would need the services of the city's ranking criminal lawyer.

"Come in and watch the fun anyway," invited Page. "We got an extra special crowd here tonight. There's one dame never been here before. She said her name was Smith, but I told the boys to let her in. Class! She's got it all over. But not much else. And is she throwing the dough! She's gone through her third stack of blue chips already!"

"I'll take a look later," said Mort without interest. "I want to pay my driver."

He went back out front, cashed one of the bills, bought his driver a drink and paid him off. Then he drank three double bourbons as fast as he could put them down. The liquor burned, but that was the only effect he got. After a while he went into the gambling room.

It was a dressed-up crowd. Mort spied the woman in the backless evening gown and guessed at once that it was she whom Page had raved about. Mort walked over to the woman and watched over her bare shoulder as she played roulette.

He watched her lose a stack of blue chips on No. 13 and said: "Mimi, even you can't afford to lose like that."

"Gambling is no fun," she replied without turning, "unless you play for more than you can afford to lose."

"But you're playing such long odds. Why don't you play a color instead of a number?"

"The hell with the red and the black. They're good only for the title of a novel."

She put another stack on 13. Mort knew that if the croupier let her win he would never turn another wheel for Lucky Page. He could have stayed there making money on the other color, but he had no desire to capitalize on the misfortune of a beautiful woman. And Mimi Carter was beautiful. Just thinking about Al Carter slopping over the table back at Milligan's made Mort feel sorry for her. He let go of her back and moved away.

He felt depressed. To think about Mimi coming here under the name of Smith and trying to kid herself into thinking she was having a thrilling time was bad enough.

But there was something more. It was deeper down. You couldn't put your finger on it, but you could feel it just the same. Mort walked back to the bar. He began to drink doubles again and this time with some seriousness.

HE WAS fairly well paralyzed when Phil Sinton, Lucky's manager, came up beside him.

"Lucky wants to see you in his office. It's important."

"Then tell Lucky to come here. I don't dare get off this bar stool, and I'm not joking."

Sinton looked at his eyes. He walked away. When he returned, Lucky was with him. He stared into Mort's face.

"My god, you are tanked! And I need you like I never needed anyone before!"

Mort had never been so drunk that he was incapable of precise, clear speech.

"What have you, Lucky?"

"A suicide. That girl I told you about. She's shot herself."

It was unnecessary for Lucky to draw a diagram. A suicide in his gambling club would close it as sure as God made little green apples. Hell would break loose in all the papers. Every one-lung reform league would take a new transfusion, and the heat would be on.

But Mort was not thinking about the imminent threat to the security of Lucky Page's club. He was thinking about how lovely Mimi Carter had looked in that backless evening gown. Mort thought it very probable that Mimi was about the most beautiful woman in the world.

"Mimi is dead," he said thickly. For the first time in many years tears that were not theatrically forced welled in Mort's eyes. Page eyed him in bafflement, then his eyes lighted.

"So you knew her, C.D.?"

"Yes. I nearly married her. But we had only one thing in common. We both agreed that she was too good for me."

"So it's like that. Well, at least you can tell me who she is."

"She's Mimi Carter. Her husband is Al Carter."

"Al—" Page stared. "Why, Al's here now! He's sleeping one off in the private room adjoining my office!" Ideas seemed to stagger him. "And this girl, his wife, she shot herself right next door!"

Mort turned slowly. "She shot herself where?"

"Just where I told you—in my office. This girl went in there to cash a check. Phil Sinton, my manager, was handling it. He left her in there for a moment, and when he came back she was lying on the floor in front of my desk. There was an automatic on the floor beside her. Right away I figured she'd done it on account of how much dough she lost. But now—"

Mort slid from his bar stool. Page grasped his arm, for he thought he was going to fall. Mort shook off his grip.

"Let go of me, Lucky. I sober up fast." He moved slowly but with amazing steadiness, and Page followed. They found Phil Sinton seated coolly upon the edge of Page's desk. He was smoking a cigarette, and a foot dangled over Mimi Carter's head.

Mort knew that he was in no condition to look at her honestly. He stared for a moment at the small automatic pistol lying a few inches from her slim, outflung hand, then he looked around until his eyes came to rest upon a door.

"Carter in there?"

Page nodded. "Go get him, Phil. This woman is his wife."

Phil Sinton's eyes widened, but only for an instant. He crossed to the door, opened it, and went inside. He closed the door behind him. Mort forced himself to look at Mimi.

"She never did this, Lucky."

"Well, she lost a lot of money. About fifteen grand."

"She had a lot more. At least a million."

"The hell you say! Who gets the dough now, Al?"

"Yes."

Page stared. "Hell, it looks like—"

"Sure, it does. Al could have done it. He could have been less drunk than he seemed. But someone else also could have done it. Who else had anything to do with her tonight?"

"I'll have Phil find out as soon as he's through with Carter."

The inner door opened, and Sinton appeared, virtually holding Carter in a standing position. Carter looked terrible. Evidently he had not been told about Mimi. He stared with glazed eyes when Sinton led him around the desk and he could see.

"Mimi! My God! What's happened to her?"

"We really aren't sure," said Mort. "She may have committed suicide. Or someone may have killed her. You had about the best opportunity to do that."

Carter looked as if he were going to be very sick.

"C.D.—you can't mean that! You can't!"

"I'm only offering the suggestion. Of course, at first blush the motive appears to be clear. By Mimi's death you inherit about a million dollars. But, on second thought, you didn't have to kill her to get at the money. You were doing all right as it was."

Carter reddened, then he turned a sickly green. He shook off Sinton and subsided into a chair.

"Don't think I didn't get the insult, C.D., because I did. But I'll let it go. I'm thinking that I need you too much to start a fight with you right now. That's because it happens that I had plenty of motive to kill Mimi. Take a look at this."

CARTER REACHED into his inside coat pocket and handed over some folded papers. Mort accepted them, looked them over with growing interest, then whistled softly.

"So Mimi's divorcing you! When were you served these papers, Al?"

"Right after you left Milligan's. Can you imagine Ned Dumont pulling a trick like that on me? It was bad enough, his taking Mimi's case against me, but to top it all off, he phoned the sheriff's office from Milligan's and had a deputy come over. Well, at least I got in one good punch before Harry and the others could stop me!"

"You mean you slugged Ned?"

"A honey! And now you're going to tell me that that adds in with everything else against me. It shows how mad I was. It shows I might have been mad enough to come here and kill Mimi. But, honest, C.D., I didn't have the slightest idea that Mimi would be here. Lucky will tell you she's never been here before."

"That's right," said Lucky. "I told you that."

Mort coolly handed back the papers.

"It does look bad for you, Al. If you're guilty, I hope you burn."

Carter's eyes widened.

"But you don't understand! I want you to take my case. I'm enough of a lawyer to know I need you."

"Not a chance, Al. Whether you killed Mimi or not, I still think you're a heel, running around with other women the way it alleges in the divorce petition. And to think Mimi turned me down because she thought I drank too much!"

Carter glared angrily. "I'd forgot, you gave her a rush once. It couldn't be you decided to frame me, could it?"

Mort took a step toward Carter, then controlled his temper. He turned on his heel, was about to leave.

Lucky Page said quickly: "Don't go, C.D. I want you to work for me. If somebody doesn't crack this case before the cops spread it all over the papers, the heat will be on. I'll pay you enough to make it interesting."

Mort studied him. "Let's see the color of your money."

Page went to his safe and opened it. He came back with a single bill.

"Here's a grand. Added to the five hundred I loaned you, that makes fifteen hundred. I'll give you back your check."

"And also a small bag of peanuts!" Mort sneered. He started for the door, ignoring the outstretched bill.

"Wait a minute. How much do you want?"

"Ten on the line, ten more if I crack this thing before the papers get it."

Page gave him an instant's murderous look, then returned to the safe and added nine bills to the one he had offered. He handed them all to Mort, who casually pocketed them, and then turned to Sinton.

"You find out who talked to Mimi here tonight."

Sinton looked to Page, who nodded. "Do anything Mr. Mort says."

Sinton left the room. A little white, Mort walked to the body, stooped and forced his gaze upon the bullet wound. It lingered there perhaps a minute, then he rose. He was a shade whiter as he turned to Carter.

"There are burns, Al. Not just powder marks and blackening, but burns. Whoever shot her held the gun within three or four inches of her face. That means it had to be someone she knew and trusted."

"O.K., she knew me, but she didn't trust me much any more. Hadn't she just filed suit for divorce?"

"Sure. But a certain amount of intimacy always lingers between divorcees. She would have let you come that close and thought nothing about it. There's nothing in the divorce petition to indicate that you ever gave her any personal injury."

"Well, I never did. Say, what about giving me a paraffin test? That will prove I haven't even fired a gun all day!"

Mort shook his head. "No, Al. Take a look at that gun. It's a new automatic. The cartridge cases fit it too snugly to permit the escape of gases carrying nitrate. The dermal nitrate test is not infallible."

"Well, I want to be tested anyway. I want the police to do it." He faced Page. "If you won't call them, I will."

Page glowered. "Make a move for that phone and see what happens."

Mort shook his head at Page. He faced Carter. "Call the cops if you like, Al, but it may not go so well with you. If you didn't kill Mimi, you'd better give me a head start before the cops give you the old third-degree."

CARTER EYED him sullenly, but he did not rise from his chair. The door opened. Mort saw Carter start and sit forward, then he turned to see why. Phil Sinton had ushered Ned Dumont into the room. Dumont stopped short at the sight of Mimi's body.

"My God! What happened to her?"

"She's been shot. What do you know about it?"

"Why, why, nothing!" Dumont's eyes shifted to Carter. "He did this! He did this, I'll bet my last dollar! She was divorcing him! He lost his temper when he was served the papers tonight, and he socked me. Then he came out here and murdered poor Mimi!"

"The hell I did!" said Carter. He got up from his chair, tottered slightly, but managed to stay on his feet. "I socked you all right, and I'll gladly sock you again. But I didn't kill Mimi. You might tell us what the hell you're doing here!"

"Yes," said Mort. "What are you doing here?"

"I came out to tell Mimi that the papers had been served. That's all. I merely spoke to her." He nodded to Sinton. "This man will tell you that."

"Sure," said Sinton. "I saw him myself. He just talked to the woman a little bit, then he went over and got into a poker game."

Dumont looked around with satisfaction. Carter's scowl did not diminish. Mort turned to Sinton. "Did Mimi talk to anyone else?"

"Yes. There was another gal about her own age. A looker, too. One of the boys spotted her being friendly with this one. He's looking for her now."

Dumont eyed Mort with curiosity. "What's going on here? Haven't the police been notified?"

"No. This is no affair of yours, Ned. Suppose you let us handle it."

"I'll do nothing of the kind! Mimi was a valued client! I'm calling the police!"

He went over to the phone on the desk and dialed. Page made a move toward him, but Mort stopped him with a look. When Dumont had put down the phone, Page said: "It's all yours, C.D. You'll have to work fast."

Mort made no comment. The door opened suddenly.

A croupier ushered a beautifully-gowned woman into the room. She was young, as had been Mimi, and very nearly as attractive. She wore a look of mingled indignation and curiosity. She saw Mimi, clapped a hand silently to her mouth.

"Hello, Nadine," said Carter. "Isn't this terrible? They think I did it on account of the divorce."

The girl stared from one to the other. Finally she said: "But there wasn't going to be any divorce, Al. Mimi told me she had decided that was what you wanted. She said she was going to withdraw the suit."

Carter stared. "When did she tell you that?"

"Just a little while ago. She had a lot of satisfaction doing it."

Mort said quietly: "I believe you're Nadine Gray. I also believe that you're the woman mentioned as correspondent in Mimi's divorce case. Am I right?"

"You are. Al and I have been in love for months. We told Mimi at the start."

"That was very noble of both of you," said Mort. "Now suppose you tell me where you've been since you talked to Mimi."

Nadine Gray looked to Al. He spoke up angrily.

"What are you trying to do, C.D.? Frame Nadine?"

"She had a good enough motive, Al. She wanted you to be free to marry her, and only by killing Mimi could she accomplish that."

Neither Al nor Nadine spoke a word. Lucky Page pointed out: "This job was done with a woman's gun, all right."

"And it could have been done by Mimi herself!" snapped Carter.

"Do you really think Mimi would pull a suicide?" Mort asked. Carter dropped his eyes. Mort turned to Page. "You could have done this yourself. So could Sinton. Have you both got an alibi ready?"

Page scowled deeply while Sinton eyed the lawyer imperturbably. "Sinton's got a perfect alibi," said Page. "He was dealing faro. I had to supervise the room. That's why I couldn't wait when Mimi Carter wanted to cash a check. I showed her to my office and came right back. A dozen guys can testify to that. Besides, what motive did I have for killing her?"

"She might have complained about her losses, threatened to start trouble."

"And you seriously think I'd commit a murder in my own club over something like that?"

"No. I'm just considering all the possibilities."

MORT FACED Dumont. "You, Ned—you had a motive. I've seen that trick form contract you have for your wealthy divorce clients. A divorce for Mimi would have netted you at least two thousand dollars. That's just about what her dropping her suit cost you. With Mimi dead you could collect the full amount from her estate."

Dumont turned slightly purple. "Why, you cheap shyster! Do you think I'd kill Mimi or anyone else for a lousy two thousand dollars? Why, my practice nets me a fifty grand a year!"

"I don't doubt that. But, as you heard me say at Milligan's, there's no limit to human pettiness, no minimum motive requirement for murder. So I'm not ruling you out. Of course, if you were in a card game, you'd have an alibi."

Dumont was no longer purple, only red. "I didn't stay in the game very long. I moved around."

Carter said quickly: "I think he's the man, C.D. Anyone petty enough to take a case against a pal wouldn't stop at anything!"

Dumont forced a laugh. "Prove it! Prove I did it!"

Mort regarded him a trifle coolly. "Oh, proving the murderer's guilt will be easy enough. I was merely trying to establish motives before I put you all to the test."

Page stepped forward. "Damn it, Mort, have you been playing with all of us, making us sit on pins and needles until you got ready to show off? If you can clinch this case before the cops get here, for crying out loud, do it!"

"Easily done. Notice, folks, the little automatic with which Mimi was shot. You will notice that it has a tiny grip. The grip is so tiny that it fits a woman's hand, but a man can get only two fingers around it. When it goes off it kicks up violently, causing the imprint of the front strap to remain for several hours on the skin of the fingers. So, if you good people will simply hold up your hands...."

"That won't be necessary!" There was no alcoholic sluggishness in Al Carter's voice now. Nor was there any clumsiness in the quick scoop of his nimble fingers as they picked up the gun from the floor.

"I'm going out of here. Don't anybody try to stop me!"

Nobody did, as he moved to the door. He reached behind him, drew the door open.

"You, Clarence Darrow Mort, have won your last murder case. You're responsible for showing me up—and you're about to get your reward for your smartness. Here goes, C.D.!"

The shot roared deafeningly. Then Carter settled quietly upon the floor.

Phil Sinton had drawn and fired so fast that by the time Carter had seen him it was too late. He growled: "Imagine that little punk thinking he could do a job like that right under my nose!"

"Nice work, Phil." Page crossed to his safe, got out another sheaf of bills, which he handed to Mort. "There it is, less the five hundred I gave you. And here's your check. It was a quick way to earn twenty grand, but you did earn it. This takes a load off my mind. By the way, before the meat wagon comes for Carter, show me those marks on his fingers you talked about."

"I doubt very much if there are any such marks," Mort yawned. "I'm afraid I cashed in on my prestige with poor Al. You see, he did have a profound respect for my knowl-edge of criminal lore. First off, I convinced him that I was an authority on the dermal nitrate test for he knew well enough that I was right. On top of that, he knew I'd tried a hundred murder cases, so when I told him the little gun would leave tell-tale marks he didn't wait to find out."

Page exchanged a quick glance with Sinton. Neither had a word to say. But Ned Dumont said: "Well, Al's being the murderer didn't illustrate your little theory that there's no minimum requirement for murder. Al had a million good reasons to kill Mimi besides Nadine here."

"True, he stood to gain a million dollars and thus insure the love of the fair Nadine—so long as the million lasted. All this would point the finger of guilt directly toward him. But tonight he had heard me expounding my theory of motive for murder. He counted on me to raise in the mind of a jury the possibility that someone else, with a horribly petty motive, might have committed the crime.

"Actually his crime illustrates my theory that no motive for murder can be too trifling. As Einstein says, all things are relative. A woman like Mimi was so wonderful that killing her for a mere million dollars is an act of ghastly pettiness."

Mort faced Nadine Gray.

"Al Carter didn't have as logical a motive for killing Mimi as he would have had if he had killed a dozen of you for a dime!"

LOADED FOR MURDER

WHAT'S IN A NAME? APPARENTLY
EVERYTHING—AT LEAST IN THE
CASE OF CLARENCE DARROW
MORT AND BLACKSTONE JONES.
TOGETHER THEY LIFTED A MAN
FROM THE HOT-SEAT AND SAW TO
IT THAT THE RIGHT PERSON GOT
THE VOLTAGE.

CLARENCE DARROW MORT alighted from his cab in front of the Baker Building, which housed his offices.

"One-fifty," said the driver. Instantly his eyes lighted as a five-dollar bill was flicked toward him with a gesture that said: "Keep the change." He repeated his fervid thanks until his fare had disappeared beyond the door of the corner drugstore.

Clarence Darrow Mort halted at the soda fountain, ordered a double dose of a nationally known acid-indigestion nostrum. He gulped down the sizzling panacea.

"That'll be ten cents," said the fountain girl.

Mort put his hand in his pocket. His fingers explored without success.

"Well, I declare! I left my money in my other clothes!"

"Mr. Oakley!" the fountain girl yelled shrilly. A dapper man with a toothbrush mustache came quickly forward. "This guy orders and he ain't got the ten cents," accused the girl.

Mr. Oakley laughed deprecatingly. He reached into his pocket and tossed a dime onto the fountain. He beamed upon Mort.

"Please overlook the incident, Mr. Mort. The girl is new here." He faced the girl with tolerant severity. "This gentlemen is Clarence Darrow Mort, the famous criminal lawyer."

The girl eyed her customer glumly.

"He didn't have the ten cents."

Mr. Oakley turned quickly back to Mort, his face reddened at such an exhibition of tactlessness by his help.

"No wonder you came out without your wallet today, Mr. Mort," he sympathized. "Losing the Brenner case must have been an awful blow to you. Why, I guess that's the first murder case you ever lost!"

Mort's face grew white. He turned on his heel and walked from the store. The manager stared while the fountain girl regarded him gloatingly. She guessed she had more tact in her little finger than the big ape had all over.

Mort reached the sidewalk and paused to breathe deeply. The ten-cent fizz had only aggravated the horrible feeling in the pit of his stomach. He had been a fool for eating that big steak at Luigi's on the south side. But then, he realized, the feeling would have been there regardless.

He walked the several steps to the building entrance, peered inside the dimly-lighted lobby. It was well after office hours, and nary a soul was in sight. Mort rose on his toes and managed to press the button that signaled the night caretaker. Presently a round little man ambled forth.

"Why, good evening, Mr. Mort! I guess I was wrong telling that young fellow you never came back after dark. Good thing he was stubborn."

Mort frowned. "What young fellow?"

"Jones is his name. He's a lawyer, so I guess it's all right I let him into the building."

Mort was too curious to remark about the inconsistency. He asked, frowning: "Where is the guy?"

The round little man looked around. "Why, he was right here a minute ago." Suddenly his face wrinkled with worry. "I told him he had to stay right here. Do you suppose he could have been lying about being a lawyer? Golly, he might be a thief!"

Mort laughed, to the caretaker's puzzlement, and walked on to the single elevator left in use. "Never mind, he probably got tired waiting and walked out."

He entered the car, and the caretaker took him to his floor. He used the door to his private office, unlocking it with his key. He had closed it before he observed his visitor. He said: "I hope I'm not intruding."

THE YOUTH occupied Mort's swivel chair, and he was making the most of it, leaning far back and propping his feet upon the polished surface of a truly distinguished walnut desk. The feet came down, but the occupant remained comfortably ensconced in the chair.

"Hello, Mr. Mort. The cleaning woman let me in. I hope you don't mind."

"Not at all. I hope you're comfortable."

The youth smiled, but with no embarrassment. "Oh, yes, I'm quite comfortable. You're probably wondering who I am. My name is Jones."

"Attorney Jones," Mort mused aloud. He crossed to a chair and subsided wearily, staring across his desk at the occupant of his own chair. His gaze was half amused, half irritated.

"Supposing you tell me what's on your mind."

"Sure, Mr. Mort. I wanted to tell you about the Brenner case."

When Clarence Darrow Mort began exploring the wound with thumb and finger, Katie McAvoy reeled, and Blackstone Jones wrested the automatic pistol from the girl's hand.

Stunned, Mort came back slowly: "You wanted to tell me about the Brenner case?"

"Yes, Mr. Mort. Of course I can see why you think that's funny, me wanting to tell you about the case when you handled it and have been trying it for the last two weeks. But I've got an idea you missed."

Mort was in no condition to exercise diplomacy. For the first time that afternoon he had heard a jury doom a client of his to the electric chair. He could not have felt worse if he had been his client. He said: "Get the hell out of here before I throw you out!"

The youth's eyes widened incredulously. He got out of Mort's chair and seemed to rise in sections. Mort stared. He had never seen a bigger man. The idea of a man of his own size, standing barely five-feet-four, throwing such a giant out of his office or anywhere else was absurd.

"But you don't understand," protested the youth. "I can tell you how to save Brenner's life! I can tell you how to get him free!"

In spite of his visitor's size, Mort rose threateningly.

"Get out, I say!" His face impressed the bigger man, for it was racked by torment. "Get out of here before I—" Mort left off helplessly. "Get out," he begged.

Moved, the youth retreated to the door. Still, he argued.

"But, Mr. Mort, I know you want to save Paul Brenner if possible. And I'm sure I can tell you how to do it!"

Mort silently implored him, and opened the door.

"All right, Mr. Mort, I'll go. But if you want to get in touch with me, you can find me at the Hotel Norwood. The name is Jones. Blackstone Jones."

The youth smiled sheepishly. "Yes, that's right. My father named me after William Blackstone. I tried to get everybody to call me 'Bill,' but somehow they always insisted on Blackstone. I guess it was just natural that I should turn out to be a lawyer."

Mort eyed him with touching sympathy.

"Come back, my boy. Sit down. I'm sorry for my lack of manners. It's just that I've taken such an awful jolt today. I really didn't mean it."

Slightly bewildered, Blackstone Jones resumed his seat in Mort's swivel chair. Mort glazed at him like a long-lost brother. He shook his head solemnly.

"We are kindred souls, Blackstone Jones. I, too, was doomed to the law by my namesake. My father was an idolator of Darrow. If I had not been named Clarence Darrow Mort, I might have turned out to be a doctor, a musician, or even a barber."

"But, Mr. Mort! You're the greatest living criminal lawyer! You should be forever grateful to your father for suggesting your destiny by naming you after Darrow, one of the greatest men of his time and certainly the greatest criminal lawyer!"

Mort shook his head forlornly.

"I envy you—if only I could share your sentiments! I'd rather drive a truck. At least I would have some peace of mind and money in my pocket. As it is, I'm a chronic nervous wreck and usually broke."

"You, broke! Why, Mr. Mort, you must make tens of thousands!"

"When my client is sufficiently well-heeled to pay—yes. But well-heeled clients do not get off every street car. Take my last client, Paul Brenner, the cab driver. When I first interviewed him in his cell he had the total sum of thirty-seven dollars in his pants. This he offered me, but I handed it back. To date I have spent a thousand dollars on private detectives who have failed to turn up either hide or hair of his mysterious missing witness. Aside from two weeks of trial work, I spent another month on the case. My overhead kept right on going. So you see me now as penniless as a vagrant, without a solitary dime in my pocket."

"But, Mr. Mort, your fee in the Brenner case has been the personal satisfaction of devoting your legal skill on behalf of a friendless, helpless man whom nobody believes! Certainly it must be a source of immeasurable pride to know that despite all odds you have fought for the freedom of an innocent man!"

Mort's brows lifted in amazement. "What—you think Brenner innocent?"

"Of course. Don't you?"

MORT SHRUGGED. Blackstone Jones nodded knowingly.

"I think I understand now why you have lost this case. You yourself do not believe in the innocence of your client. Why, then, did you defend him with no hope of payment?"

"Because, my lad, I can feel for the guilty as well as the innocent. The constitution of our country provides that every accused man shall be entitled to counsel. It is part of the Bill of Rights. And there's nothing there that says the right belongs only to the innocent. It's the right of the guilty as well."

"But, I'm sure Brenner's innocent! Consider his story. On the night of October 18th, last, he was waiting at his usual stand outside the Lucky Club when the doorman whistled. Brenner pulled up for his fare, who was Oliver Hayworth.

"Brenner knew Hayworth, as did almost everybody in town, for he was its richest man. Outside of his manufacturing interests he had many others, principally real estate, though he dabbled in anything he could make money out of. He was no miser—he just got a personal satisfaction out of making money. He didn't need it to spend on himself or anybody else. He just wanted to make money.

"Brenner was elated at picking up such a fare, especially when Hayworth told him he had just won five thousand dollars at the Lucky Club. It was foolish of Hayworth to tell this to a strange cab driver, but he was pretty drunk. All this Brenner admitted when the police arrested him the next morning. Hayworth's body had been found in a vacant lot on the south side of town. He had been clubbed to death, and his pockets had been emptied.

"Brenner was, of course, charged with the murder. He protested his innocence, saying that he had dropped

Hayworth downtown in the vicinity of the Weems Hotel, a cheap place with a shady reputation. But circumstances were not in Brenner's favor. When the police walked in he was packing all his belongings. And a frisk of his clothes produced a one thousand-dollar bill.

"Brenner's explanation was simple but hardly convincing. When Hayworth had paid his fare, he said, he had tossed the bill and told him to keep the change. It had been a shock to find that it was a thousand-dollar bill. Brenner's reaction was one of mingled joy and panic. Surely Hayworth would regret his generosity when he sobered and claim that he had made a mistake in tossing Brenner such a huge bill. He would want it back.

"So Brenner decided to get out of town. This was his story, and he was stuck with it because he immediately weakened it by promising to prove it by a witness, another fare whom he had picked up as he had left Hayworth near the Weems.

"This second fare was also a drunk, and he had said merely that he had wanted to go home. He gave an address, which Brenner remembered, for remembering addresses had become a habit with him. The police could easily check the address, 1225 Summit Road. They found the house bearing that number to be occupied by an aged couple, neither of whom had any knowledge of a younger man answering Brenner's description of his fare. Am I correct, Mr. Mort, in saying that it was the failure of Brenner's corroborating evidence which undermined whatever credibility his story might have possessed?"

"Correct, Jones. Once the D.A. had proved Brenner a liar with respect to the second fare, the jury refused to believe any part of his story."

"That is why, Mr. Mort, I think I can save Paul Brenner's life. I am positive that I can produce the missing fare."

Mort sat up straight.

"Go on."

"Being a stranger in the city, I am unfamiliar with its streets. Parenthetically, I tell you that my sole reason for visiting it was to complete my legal education by seeing you in action.

"In order to listen intelligently to the trial I wanted to know something about the locale of the crime. For example, I wanted to know where the Lucky Club was, so I went out and spent an evening there. The better to inform myself I bought a city directory and map.

"It wasn't until today during the district attorney's final argument that I made what I believe to be an important discovery. I was idly fingering the directory, and my eyes traveled down the list of streets. Summit Road was already check-marked. But now, for the first time, I noticed that immediately after it was listed Sunbary Avenue. Hastily, I turned the pages of the directory, discovered that there is an address, 1225 Sunbary Avenue."

Mort relaxed in his chair, his face falling with disappointment.

"So you think Brenner, a seasoned cab driver, could have mistaken instructions to go to Sunbary Avenue for instructions to go to Summit Road?"

"I do. And I have already some proof that he did. I visited 1225 Sunbary Avenue this evening. It is a boarding house. The landlady was most cooperative. One of her tenants answers the description of Brenner's missing fare. And, the lady confided, the man is quite a drinker. Of course she couldn't remember whether he had been drunk on the night of October 18. But, if he wasn't, she says, it was a red-letter day in his life."

THE HOUSE numbered 1225 Sunbary Avenue was a large, rambling one. Alighting from the cab, Mort eyed it speculatively.

"Understand, Jones, that I'm on this wild-goose chase against my better judgment. If Brenner had actually misunderstood the address given him by his drunken fare and delivered him over on the other side of town on Summit Road as a result, the fare would have had to travel about five miles to get here. He would have remembered the mistake. And he would have come forward after all the newspaper publicity about the missing witness."

Blackstone Jones shook his head.

"Not necessarily. In the first place, the man was drunk. Drunk enough not to speak plainly when he uttered the name of the street he lived on. And very probably drunk enough to take another five-mile ride without remembering it. Besides, even if he did realize that he was the missing witness, his unflattering description in the newspapers would not encourage him to come forward. He might have had ridicule as his reward, possibly even the loss of his job, for this prospective witness happens to be a newspaperman himself. Maybe you know him, Eddie Davis."

Mort stopped short at the foot of the veranda steps.

"Then let's go back right now. Sure I know Eddie Davis. He's a court reporter for the *Standard*. And he covered the Brenner trial. He even interviewed Brenner in his cell. Do you think Brenner wouldn't have identified him?"

Blackstone Jones also halted. He stared down at the older lawyer.

"You—you're sure?"

"Of course I'm sure! And I'm also sure that even if Brenner had failed to recognize Davis, Davis himself would have had his memory jogged and would have placed Brenner before the long-winded trial was over. Sorry, Jones, but what I hoped would be a long-shot coming through seems just to be a coincidence."

Blackstone Jones looked like a crestfallen little boy in spite of his size. Then his jaw hardened.

"But, still, Mr. Mort, I think it's not just coincidence. I still want to talk to Davis!"

"Well, you'll have your chance. Here he comes now."

Blackstone Jones turned. A flashy crimson convertible had pulled up at the curb, though the crimson of the car was dulled by the flaming red hair of the girl driving it. Blackstone Jones could not hold back a low whistle.

"If you can take your eyes off Katie McAvoy," said Mort, "the guy with her is Eddie Davis."

The man got out of the car. "I won't be long," he said. He was a man not very much out of the ordinary, except that he was obviously much older than the red-top. She couldn't have been over twenty-two. Mort noted the frown on his youthful companion's face and smiled.

"It's the manpower shortage. Eddie's a squirt compared to most of Katie's admirers at the Lucky Club. She sings there."

Blackstone Jones nodded with enthusiasm. "I know, I know! I saw her the night I was there. She's wonderful!"

Mort gave him a quick glance, then smiled as Davis came up the walk.

"Hello, Eddie. We were just coming to see you."

Davis stared at Blackstone Jones. Mort said: "This is Attorney Jones, from out of town. He's got an interesting slant on the Brenner case. He says you're the mysterious missing witness."

Davis' eyes popped. He laughed.

"That's good!" He grinned at Blackstone Jones. "What crystal ball have you been looking into, Tarzan?"

Something in Blackstone Jones' face made Davis take a backward step, put up a hand in mock defense and add quickly: "Take it easy, guy! I couldn't help making the crack—you're about the biggest guy I've seen in a long while, especially since the draft."

Instantly, Blackstone Jones was on the defensive.

"I'm an inch too tall for the army. The limit is six-feet-six. I tried to scrunch down, but—"

"Sure, sure," said Davis in a very friendly manner. "You can't help being out of the army any more than I can. With me it's the old blood pressure."

"Then you shouldn't drink," Blackstone Jones said severely. "Were you drinking on the night of Hayworth's murder?"

Davis looked blankly at Mort. Mort grinned. Davis looked back at his inquisitor.

"Listen, fellow, that's none of your business! And what's more, I don't like this gag about me being the missing witness, the guy Brenner says he hauled. Whatever gave you that idea?"

Mort sighed. "The street address Brenner gave as his fare's destination. It's the same as yours, only on Summit. Jones thinks Brenner might have made a mistake and dumped you out on the wrong street."

"And then didn't spot me all through the trial? Are you crazy?"

"No, Eddie, just desperate. They're going to fry Brenner. That won't be good for my business."

"Well, I hope you come up with a better idea than this one. Me, the missing witness—that's good!"

He went on into his rooming house. Mort nodded to Blackstone Jones, and they went down the walk.

"Katie," said Mort, walking up to the crimson car, "I want you to meet one of your most ardent admirers. He caught your act at the Lucky Club, and he thinks you're wonderful. The name is Jones—one of the Jones boys."

Blackstone Jones' face was almost as red as Katie McAvoy's hair. She smiled and said: "Thanks for the plug."

Blackstone Jones came through with a lot of silence. Mort said casually: "You wouldn't happen to be on your way to the Lucky Club now, would you? If you are, you can give us a lift."

"Sure, climb in back. Eddie just went in to pick up something. He'll be right out."

DAVIS WAS almost on the run as he came out of his rooming house. He slowed unhappily when he saw the passengers in the convertible's rear seat.

"We're not going downtown, C.D. We're going to the Lucky Club."

"So are we, Eddie. Climb in."

Davis didn't like it. He slammed the door hard and had barely a word to say all the way. At the Lucky Club he saw to it that Katie McAvoy had no opportunity to linger in the vicinity of Blackstone Jones. Mort led the youth straight past the bar, never once faltering. Three bartenders looked stunned.

Inside the gambling room, to which the pair was immediately admitted, Mort cast a roving glance. His gaze stopped at a man who seemed to be concentrating on the play at a roulette table. A keen observer would have noted that his eyes had the split-vision cultivated by basketball players who can observe the entire floor. This was demonstrated when Mort nodded and the man came immediately in answer to his nod.

"Good evening, Mr. Mort. You're a little early today."

"I didn't come to lose my shirt this time, Phil. I want to see Lucky."

Phil Sinton enjoyed his employer's confidence because of his careful discretion.

"Certainly, Mr. Mort. I don't know if Mr. Page has come in yet, but I'll see."

Sinton vanished through a corridor, returned a minute later.

"Go right in, Mr. Mort."

"Thanks. Will you come along, Phil? You're really the man I want to talk to."

A short corridor led to the Lucky Club office. It was as sumptuously furnished as the inner sanctum of a movie mogul, and the occupant of the high-backed chair at a hand-carved desk looked at home. He smiled a warm welcome that indicated he had been seeing a lot of Edward Arnold movies lately. He kept in character throughout the introductions.

"Always glad to see you, C.D. What can I do for you now?"

"Just tell Phil that he can answer one question. I want to know if Eddie Davis was here the night of the Hayworth murder."

Only the shell of Page's smile remained.

"What's your angle, C.D.? I don't like a tie-up between the club and that Hayworth thing. Just because he'd won five grand here before he got bumped is no reason for dragging the club into the picture."

"Of course not, Lucky. But the jury hung it on Brenner this afternoon. Perhaps you had heard."

"I heard. That's bad for you, C.D. Your first loser, isn't it?"

"I haven't counted it lost yet. That's why I'm interested in Eddie's whereabouts the night of the murder. A court reporter of a paper like the *Standard* would be noticed. Phil would remember him if he was here. That's all I want to know."

Page thought this over a moment, then gave Sinton an expressive look.

Sinton said: "He wasn't here, Mr. Mort. That's definite."

"Well, that's that." Mort rose, and Blackstone Jones took his cue. Then Mort paused.

"By the way, the dealer that Hayworth won the money from, is he around?"

Page said: "He comes on at ten."

Mort chuckled, as if to himself. "I thought maybe you'd canned him, Lucky. I didn't suppose any dealer in the world could give away five grand of your money and hang up his hat here again."

Page shrugged. "I charged it up to advertisement, C.D. Besides, Hayworth was having a hot streak. Everybody has a hot streak if they gamble long enough. Sooner or later they cool off. I figured Hayworth'd give us back our money and maybe a little bit more. But it wasn't in the cards—he got picked up by the wrong cab. That's why I hope they do fry Brenner, C.D. That was my money he stole."

"So it wasn't just a hit and run? Hayworth had a hot streak, did he?"

"Yeah. The week before he got killed he came in here and took the dice game for three grand. That makes eight he took me for."

Mort smiled. "If I were a cynical man, Lucky, I might think two and two tied you with the Hayworth kill." Mort added quickly: "But I'm not cynical."

Lucky Page leaned forward in his chair.

"I don't like that, C.D."

"And I don't either!" snapped Phil Sinton. He took two steps forward and towered over the lawyer. Mort understood perfectly well that Sinton was merely putting on a loyalty act to impress his boss, but Blackstone Jones didn't. Before Sinton knew what was happening to him, he was hoisted from the floor.

Sinton swore. His hand clutched in impotent fury toward the left lapel of his coat, for Blackstone Jones, whatever the naivete that had prompted him to maltreat Sinton, saw to it that the man could not reach his armpit hardware.

Lucky Page sat wide-eyed. "What the hell, C.D.? Tell the big guy to put Phil down. He didn't mean it!"

Mort laughed. "Put him down, Jones. And you, Lucky, tell your muscleman to keep away from me!"

Page chose to laugh it off as Sinton's feet again rested on the floor. Sinton's face was scarlet, and his fingers quivered. They did not, however, reach under his coat-lapel. Mort lifted himself from his chair.

"Come along, Jones. It's time we got out of here."

This time Mort did not pass the bar. He lifted an eyebrow to Blackstone Jones.

"By the way, I haven't had a drink today. Frankly, this Brenner thing got me down so bad that I knew a drink wouldn't help. But now my spirits are picking up. Unfortunately, however, I happen to be financially embarrassed. I—"

"I'd be delighted to buy you a drink," said Blackstone Jones, "though I never touch the stuff myself."

Mort surveyed him with appreciative thoughtfulness.

"I respect your abstinence, Jones. Also your generosity. I wonder if your offer to buy a drink could be construed to mean a double."

"Of course, Mr. Mort."

BLACKSTONE JONES watched with mingled disapproval and respect at the speed with which the criminal lawyer downed a double bourbon. Mort licked his lips, happened to think of appearances and piously took a sip from his chaser.

"What do you think now?" Blackstone Jones asked. "Do you still think the use of the same street number was just a coincidence?"

Mort shrugged. "Perhaps, if subconscious motivation is not outlawed from the realm of coincidence. But suppose we occupy ourselves with more pleasant pursuits. The early show is about to begin. Move up a little closer."

The lights had been lowered. A master of ceremonies stepped forth and began to play with a microphone.

"Ladies and gentlemen," he announced, after telling two borderline jokes, "I regret to have to tell you that our lovely songstress, Miss Katie McAvoy, who usually appears at this time to do her inimitable numbers, has been unable to reach the club owing to a benefit performance at a well-known charitable institution. However, Miss McAvoy will make the next show."

The master of ceremonies then launched into another story, while Blackstone Jones turned uncomprehendingly to Mort.

"Why, Mr. Mort, that's a downright lie! We know Miss McAvoy came here!"

"Indeed we do. It would seem that the redheaded lady has departed. That being the case, I think we are wasting our time here. Suppose we go back to the gambling room, Jones."

"But, Mr. Mort, you have no money, and I don't gamble."

"I'm still gambling, Jones." He checked his watch. "Brownie Coombs comes on at ten. It's about that now. I'd like a word with Brownie."

The two men skirted the night club, reentered the gambling room. Mort affected an interest in a dice game while Blackstone Jones looked on disdainfully, but with ill-concealed curiosity. After ten minutes Mort checked his watch. Brownie Coombs had not appeared at his blackjack table. Spying Sinton, Mort crossed to him casually.

"Brownie's a little late, isn't he?"

"He's not coming. He called in and said he had a cold."

"That's a shame. Would you mind giving me his address?"

"Not at all. The Marbury Arms. Know where that is?"

"Sure."

In a phone booth, Mort learned at the expense of a borrowed nickel that Brownie Coombs was not in at the Marbury Arms, that he had gone out an hour ago and had not stated when he would be back, Mort returned to the bar, looked so longingly at the array of bottles that

Blackstone Jones offered him another drink. The offer was accepted.

"Coincidence," said Mort, when he had downed the double, "is a strange thing. When it becomes common. I'm inclined to wonder if it isn't design in disguise. Now, I've just found that Brownie Coombs is among the missing. So is Katie McAvoy. I wonder if anybody has seen Eddie Davis."

A bartender looked up.

"Eddie went out of here twenty minutes ago, Mr. Mort."

"Well, there you are! All three of them missing. Now I'd like to know if such a coincidence isn't synthetic."

"Something's up, Mr. Mort. I'm sure of it"

"Me, too. I think it calls for another drink."

Blackstone Jones looked pained but acquiesced. Mort saw a bartender coming, and he was about to order when the man said: "There's a call for you, Mr. Mort. The middle booth."

When Mort answered, a voice said: "I'm at the Weems, Room 408. If you want the low-down on the Hayworth thing, come on the run."

The connection was broken. Mort went back to the bar. A drink awaited him.

"Never mind that drink, though thanks for ordering. I hope you've got more cab-fare."

Outside they had to wait. From the parking lot a torpedo-bodied sedan rolled into the street, headed past them downtown.

"Dammit," said Mort, "he might have picked us up. It was Phil Sinton."

"Where are we going?"

"The Weems Hotel. I just got a call from there. It was Brownie Coombs. He's ready to sing."

Blackstone Jones trembled with excitement. "Then we've got to get there! Somebody may try to stop him!"

"Well, unless you want to carry me there piggy-back, it looks as if there's nothing we can do about it."

It was ten minutes before the Lucky Club doorman could whistle down a cab. "Give him a dollar," said Mort. Blackstone Jones handed over a bill as if it were the end of his finger. He appeared to brood over the tip all the way to the Weems.

"Keep the change," said Mort, when the youth handed over a five in front of the Weems. He might have had a rebellion on his hands if Mort hadn't called his attention to the crimson convertible parked near the hotel entrance.

"Looks as if Brownie has visitors. Let's go."

The clerk asked no questions as they walked to the elevator. At the fourth floor Mort led the way down a rear corridor. At No. 408 he rapped on the panels vigorously. There was no answer.

Mort tried the door. It opened easily.

"Oh, my!" said Blackstone Jones.

The girl had red hair and an automatic pistol.

"All right," she said, "come in, both of you. And don't make a row."

"Delighted," said Mort. He held the door until Blackstone Jones had entered, then closed it. "You seem to be quite a gal, Katie. Are you responsible for that, too?"

SHE DIDN'T follow the direction of his gaze. Blackstone Jones was already staring, wide-eyed, at the man trussed up on the bed. The man's throat was cut, and his head lay back making the gash appear like a second mouth.

"Don't talk nonsense!" snapped Katie McAvoy. "How could I have tied him up like that and put him there?"

"If you didn't, who did?"

"How would I know? I just got here."

"Of course the clerk downstairs will verify that."

"He won't. I got the room number wrong—I thought Brownie said it was 508. I wandered around on the fifth floor for fifteen minutes. Then I tried this floor. The door was open, and Brownie was like that."

"That," said Mort, "is not a very nice way to be."

He walked over to the dead man. He stooped slightly. Then, without hesitation, he began to explore the gaping wound with his thumb and finger.

"My God!" said Katie McAvoy. She reeled. Blackstone Jones had also been shocked by Mort's behavior. But he recovered in time to wrest the automatic pistol from the girl's hand. Despite her make-up, she was white. She turned her back to the bed. Blackstone Jones steadied her.

Mort finished what he was doing. He took several bloodied fragments of paper that he had removed from Coombs' throat and spread them on a stand. He flattened them out and put them together like a crossword puzzle. Then he scrutinized his assembled work for some minutes. He then turned about, found a wall phone and dialed. When he got an answer he asked for Captain Randolph of Homicide.

"Sorry to bother you at this hour," Mort told him. "But you can crack two murder cases with one stone if you get Paul Brenner and bring him over to the Lucky Club. I'll meet you in Lucky's office."

He turned from the phone, carefully picked up the gory pieces of his jig-saw puzzle. He emptied a legal-size envelope from his inside coat pocket and tucked in the pieces. Then he eyed Blackstone Jones.

"The gun, Jones. I'll handle that."

He accepted the proffered gun, gripped it with his left hand and jacked back the slide. No cartridge popped out. Mort laughed.

"Why, it wasn't even loaded!"

"Of course not! I don't even know how to shoot one of those things!"

"Then why did you carry it?"

"I don't have to tell you."

Mort shrugged. "Suit yourself. You'll have to tell Captain Randolph. You're coming with us to Lucky's office."

She showed no sign of resistance. Mort found the "Do Not Disturb" sign, hung it on the outside doorknob, doused the lights and locked the door upon the room. Downstairs, he led the way to the red convertible.

"You can drive us, Katie. A snazzy car for a chirp, if you ask me."

"You may as well know. It's not mine. It belongs to Eddie Davis."

Mort's brows lifted. "That's still more surprising! A newspaper reporter makes more money than I thought."

Katie McAvoy drove away sullenly. She parked in the Lucky Club lot, and they used the rear entrance. Lucky Page had evidently been advised of their arrival. He met them as they came out of the kitchen.

"We want to use your office," said Mort. "Captain Randolph's on his way with Paul Brenner. You can help us by rounding up Phil Sinton. Also Eddie Davis, if he should happen to pop in."

Neither man had put in an appearance fifteen minutes later when Randolph, accompanied by two detectives, arrived with his prisoner. They crowded into Page's office.

"Now, if you guys will just tell me what this is all about," Page said.

Mort nodded. "Sure. It's about murder. When it strikes once, it's apt to strike twice, like tonight."

"Twice?" Randolph looked down his nose.

"Brownie Coombs," said Mort. "He got it in Number 408 at the Weems Hotel."

"Then, why—"

"Skip it, Randolph," Mort interrupted him. "You'll get your killer this way. Here's the only piece of evidence that was in that room. I fished it out of Brownie's throat."

Katie McAvoy looked on in horror as Mort handed over the envelope.

"It was terrible! How could you have done such a thing?" She got a handkerchief out of her bag and dabbed her eyes. Randolph began to spread the contents of the envelope on Page's desk, to the consternation of the latter. When he had finished assembling the pieces he read them and whistled.

"This is the pay-off! I can't read all of it on account of the blood, but I can read enough!" he said to Mort.

Then he turned on Paul Brenner. "What do you know about this affidavit?"

THE CAB driver was a thin, beaten-down man of forty-five. His gray, haggard face trembled. He stared from Randolph to Mort.

"What do I know about what?"

"The affidavit," Mort told him, "states that on a night about a week before Hayworth's murder you hauled Hayworth to his home. Is that right, Brenner?"

Brenner looked bewildered. "Maybe, Mr. Mort. I'd hauled Hayworth several times. Like I told you, I had my stand here at the Lucky Club."

"Do you remember on one particular night after you had hauled Hayworth, your next fare was Eddie Davis? You should remember, for the affidavit states that Davis asked you who your last fare was, and you told him it was Hayworth. Now, does that help?"

Brenner's brow wrinkled, then he suddenly nodded.

"Come to think of it, I do remember. I took Davis home."

"Exactly. What you never knew was the reason for Davis' curiosity about your previous fare. He had found a pair of dice on the floor of your cab. The next day he learned two things. One was that the dice were wrong—that Hayworth had won three thousand dollars at the Lucky Club the night before.

"Eddie Davis knew that he had something. He sat down at his typewriter and dictated an affidavit, which the office notary signed. He had an idea Hayworth wouldn't care to have the contents of that affidavit made public.

"He knew Hayworth was a hard nut to crack. (I'm going on pure supposition now.) However, a couple of days later, Hayworth received a visit. The visitor was almost apologetic in making reference to the wrong dice and the existence of an affidavit. The visitor used the technique of all blackmailers. The victim was made to believe that the blackmailer was a friend, that in the end the victim would actually make a profit out of the transaction.

"The blackmailer voiced an understanding disposition and a desire to assist Hayworth in taking Lucky Page's games. For example, the blackmailer had won a little money at the friendly blackjack table at which Brownie Coombs dealt. Not much money, because both Lucky Page and Phil Sinton knew the blackmailer was friendly with Brownie, and they would quickly smell a rat if the thing were carried too far.

"But a man like Hayworth would be above suspicion— that was why he had been able to get away with those wrong dice. The stick man would have palmed them if anybody else had made that many passes. Now, if Hayworth played blackjack with the benefit of some code words, the three of them would split a nice piece of loot.

"Hayworth understood perfectly. He was getting off easy. If he didn't comply with the blackmailer's wish, the situation would become embarrassing. If he did, it wouldn't cost anything, and he would make some money besides. So he practiced up on Brownie's code words and went back to the Lucky Club for a whirl at blackjack.

"He won five thousand, and left in Brenner's cab, for Brenner was at his usual stand. The thing had got Hayworth's nerves, and he had stopped first at the bar. He was in such a drunken condition that he gave Brenner a thousand-dollar bill instead of what he probably thought was a ten. Brenner rightly surmised that his fare had made a mistake, and he made ready to leave town before Hayworth sobered up.

"Now picture Hayworth visiting a room at the Weems Hotel, the room in which he was to meet the blackmailer. He's ready to split the loot, but the blackmailer says there has been a slight change in plans. The loot is to be split, all right, but Hayworth will not be a party to it. The money Hayworth was to hand over now was only the beginning.

"Hayworth got the idea. The affidavit about the dice hadn't been very much against him, but now there was plenty. There were witnesses of his conspiracy to defraud Page. A thing like that might not be pushed in a criminal court, but Lucky Page had a way of settling his own scores. If Hayworth decided to face the music, the blackmailer and Brownie Coombs could get out of town quickly enough, but Hayworth's manifold investments were there, and he had to stay.

"The blackmailer had known Hayworth would be a tough nut to crack, but not how tough. Hayworth came to a quick decision. He walked to the wall phone and began to dial police headquarters. The blackmailer came to another quick decision. Hayworth was struck down before he could make the call. Afterwards the blackmailer and Brownie Coombs dumped the body in a south-side lot. That's the story, Randolph."

Randolph nodded. "It sounds convincing to me, C.D., but it's all theory. The affidavit is the only fact we have to go on."

"It's enough. Get Eddie Davis in here, and I'll wrap it up."

There was a rap on the door. A detective admitted Phil Sinton.

"Where have you been?" Randolph demanded.

Sinton replied: "The Weems Hotel. Brownie phoned me. Lucky will tell you that."

"Brownie's dead," said Lucky dully. Sinton nodded.

"I know," he said. "I took a glim at the room and got out."

"What did Brownie want to see you about?"

"I don't know. But I'm sure it was plenty."

"Where have you been since?"

"Looking for Eddie Davis."

"You find him?"

"Sure. He's at the bar."

"Why were you looking for him, Phil?"

"He was a pal of Brownie's. I thought maybe he might know something."

Randolph spoke to a detective. "Bring him in."

EDDIE DAVIS looked calm and carefree.

"This is quite a party. I hope there's a good story in it."

"There will be," said Mort. "Did you know Brownie Coombs was murdered?"

"The hell he was!"

"Take a look at this affidavit, Eddie. Tell us if you've ever seen it before."

Davis whitened as he spied the fragments.

"Wh—where did you find that?"

"In Brownie's throat," said Mort. "He had eaten it."

Davis trembled. "You can't tie me in with this—or with Hayworth's murder! I had nothing to do with either one."

"Oh, yes you did," said Mort grimly. "That affidavit was used to blackmail Hayworth. When that deal went haywire, the same affidavit was used again. This time on Brownie. Brownie had decided to bow out of the deal. Though he'd helped dispose of the body, there's no such thing as an accessory after the fact in this state, and he'd have immunity for turning state's evidence. He was worried about Lucky's reaction, so he called Sinton to the Weems as well as me. But Hayworth's murderer smelled a rat and killed him."

"You might get off with life," said Randolph, "if you confess now. It's the best way."

"Are you crazy?" Mort barked at Randolph. "Davis had the affidavit, didn't he?"

"No I didn't! It was gone when I tried to find it this evening!"

Randolph laughed in his face, but Mort said: "I believe you Eddie. That should teach you never to smuggle red-headed ladies into your room. You did tell Katie about that affidavit shortly after you signed it, didn't you?"

Davis' face froze. Mort went on.

"Sure, Eddie, I know you got cold feet and dropped the idea of blackmailing Hayworth. But when you told Katie about it, she put it to work. She killed Hayworth, and tonight she took care of Brownie, making him eat that affidavit so it would point directly to you! She asked you to get it for her this evening to put you off guard, didn't she?"

"You're a liar!" Katie McAvoy jumped out of her chair. "You can't prove anything on me! I went to Brownie's room when he called me. I had a gun when you walked in because I was frightened. The gun's Eddie's."

Mort shook his head. "That's not good enough, Katie. The gun's probably Eddie's, but it's not the one you used when you made him eat that affidavit. And it's not the one you used when you made him turn around so you could slug him. Where you got the knife, I don't know, but I will."

Katie McAvoy's hand darted into her purse. It was full of automatic pistol when it emerged.

"I really know how to use one of these, Mort. And this one's loaded!"

"So's the one in my pocket," said Mort.

Katie McAvoy glanced long enough at Mort's bulging pocket to permit Randolph to twist the automatic from her hand.

At the bar, Phil Sinton told Mort: "What I don't understand, was where Katie was when I looked into that room."

"Behind the door, probably. If you'd made the mistake of entering, you'd probably have been Suspect Number Two, Eddie."

Eddie Davis said: "And to think I hocked everything I owned for that red-headed cluck!"

"Now, now," said Mort. "Be careful not to speak ill of ladies, for we all are the pawns of Lady Luck."

"I see what you mean," said Blackstone Jones. "Without pure coincidence, you'd never have cracked the Hayworth case. The coincidence was that Brenner told you he'd taken a fare to the same address on Summit as Davis has on Sunbary."

Mort shook his head. "That's not a very pure variety of coincidence. Brenner's use of the same street address was not luck. It was the working of his subconscious. He had hauled Hayworth a week before, then hauled Davis home. When he had to fake a story for his alibi, the sequence of events had remained in his mind, though he had forgotten the facts themselves. The number popped out of his subconscious, and Sunbary Avenue came to him in disguise as Summit Road. Have you ever read Freud?"

Jones shook his head. "No, but I will."

"I hope you have time enough. After this case the firm of Mort & Jones will probably be very busy."

"You mean—why—that will be wonderful! I'll be Boswell to your Johnson, Arthur Train to your Tutt!"

"Be careful," counseled Mort, "not to get your Tutt caught!"

CORPUS DELICTI DE LUXE

"AND THAT" SAID THE DISTRICT ATTORNEY, "IS PERRY COURTNEY'S CONFESSION TO MURDER. I ASK THE COURT THAT IT BE ADMITTED AS STATE'S EXHIBIT NUMBER ONE." "AND I OBJECT," SAID CLARENCE DARROW MORT. "YOU NEED MORE THAN A CONFESSION. WHERE'S THE BODY? WHERE'S THE HANDKERCHIEF THAT WIPED THE BLOOD AWAY? WHERE'S THE EVIDENCE THAT THERE WAS EVER ANY BLOOD ON THAT LINOLEUM?" "OBJECTION SUSTAINED," SAID THE JUDGE. "I ORDER THE JURY TO RETURN A VERDICT OF NOT GUILTY!" AND THAT SEEMED TO BE THAT—EXCEPT THAT THE BODY TURNED UP FIVE MINUTES AFTER ACQUITTAL.

CHAPTER ONE
AND THE GUILTY
SHALL GO FREE

THE BACK door was locked and there wasn't any answer when I knocked. That didn't necessarily mean Moran wasn't in his office. Visitors were supposed to come via the front way, past the hotel clerk's desk and only after the clerk had checked with Moran by phone. But I'd used the back door so often that I'd developed a certain little *rat-a-tat* that Moran had got to know. Only he might be pretending not to recognize it now. He had plenty of reason.

It was stated in bold letters on the placard I carried in my hand. I'd torn it from a post on the boardwalk the moment I'd spotted it. I knew the thing was no typographical error. It meant what it said. Moran was going to run Dance Palace every night through the season, and he hadn't even bothered to ask my leave. There were reasons why he should—fifty thousand of them.

That was my investment in Dance Palace, the big closed pavilion that stood at the far end of Jim Moran's boardwalk. Moran owned everything else accessible from the boardwalk—the gyp games, the lunch stands, the shooting gallery, the night club, the hotel and its fancy cocktail lounge. He had by far the biggest holdings at Prescott Lake, billed throughout the mid-west as its "Billion Dollar Playground." Only it was my dough in Dance Palace.

All Moran had put up was the spot, the location. He'd operated a small pavilion there for years, but the fire marshal was about to condemn it so he sold me the idea of going into partnership and putting up the dough for a big new layout. The way he sold the idea made it sound good. According to him I'd get my fifty grand back in five years, and from then on I'd net a clear ten grand a year.

That had been two years ago. At the time I hadn't been completely taken in by Moran's sales talk, but there had been a sound reason in the back of my mind for throwing in with him.

Anyone with eyes and the proper viewpoint could see what my reason was. Micky Moran, Jim's daughter, was the bait that got me, whether Jim realized it or not. Thinking it over, the odds are long that he did. I'll bet my shirt on it.

I'd almost lost my shirt in the two years since. Things generally had gone sour with me. About everything I could call my own was tied up in the Palace. And the Palace definitely wasn't the money-maker Jim Moran had cracked it up to be.

He kept saying the fault lay in the war. So many fellows had been drafted that the girls didn't have anybody to dance with but themselves, and they didn't like that so much. Whatever it was, the Palace was dancing about

He lay in his own bathtub, head back against the faucet. "Well, this time we've got a *corpus delicti,* C.D.," Blackie Jones said.

thirty couples on the average through the week. With what we were paying the band and all the rest of the overhead, it took thirty-six couples on the floor to break even.

Saturday nights and Sundays we played to fair crowds. Even then the profit wasn't so much, but we were making money two days out of the week. So this year I'd gone to Moran and said: "I'm cutting out the weekday dancing. The Palace is going to run only on Saturdays and Sundays. That way I can at least buy groceries, which is more than I was able to do out of the proceeds last year. That all right by you?"

Moran hit the ceiling.

"The hell it's all right! The Palace is going to stay open every summer night! Do you think I want a blackout at the end of the walk? Hell, that's what pulls the people the whole length!"

"Sure," I mollified, "I know the Palace is a feeder for your concessions. But it's no feeder for me while it runs at a loss. You've got all the rest of your stuff to live off—you can afford to take a loss on the Palace just to feed the walk. Me, I've just got the Palace, and I aim to see that it makes me some dough this summer."

Moran eyed me calmly now. He was fifty, and he'd had plenty of ups and downs all his life. He'd handled many a situation, and now he started out to handle this one.

"Perry, do yourself a favor. Don't try to monkey with the Palace this summer or any other summer. If you do, you won't come out so good."

IT BURNED me up. I turned on my heel, walked to my car and drove into the city to see my lawyer. He was an old pal of mine, Hank Sloan. I showed him my partnership contract with Moran. He looked it over and frowned.

"Perry, why the hell didn't you let me see this contract before you signed it?"

"You were out of town, Hank. I took it for granted Moran was on the level, and I didn't hire a lawyer. His own lawyer, Bob Cartel, drew up the contract. You sound like I'm hooked. Am I?"

"I'm afraid so. The contract doesn't definitely say the Palace is to stay open every night through the season, but it does say you're to receive a salary for operating it through the season. The implication isn't too plain, but it's there."

"But, if I'm to operate, can't I say when the doors open?"

"Not necessarily. If a certain general policy is outlined in the contract you can't, as manager, change that policy. But the question isn't very definitely answered. A court might say the facts justified your closing through the week."

"But you're not sure?"

"No."

"And you think the odds are against that?"

"Frankly, yes."

I picked up my contract and drove back to Prescott Lake.

"I've seen a lawyer," I bluffed. "The Palace is dark through the week."

"The hell it is," said Moran. "I've seen my lawyer, too. The Palace stays open all season!"

I kept up the bluff, hiring a band to play two nights only and matinees on Sundays. Then, this afternoon, I'd chanced to see Hal Caldwell in town. Hal had led the band at Moran's night club the year before.

"You're a little early, Hal. The club doesn't open till Decoration Day."

Hal grinned in a superior manner. "Yeah, I know. But the Palace opens next week, and I'm opening there."

I kept my temper. I made a bee-line for the boardwalk. When I got there I saw the first of Moran's placards advertising the Palace opening, the one I still carried in my hand.

If Moran was in his office, he wasn't going to open up, at least the back door, so I went around front through the hotel. Amy Milroy was at the desk. She told me Moran hadn't come through that way, and I knew Amy wouldn't kid me. I left the hotel and went down the boardwalk toward Prescott Street, the one and only business street in town.

The boardwalk was pretty well deserted, for it hadn't opened up. I recognized a familiar figure puttering about one of the concessions.

"Hello, Happy," I said.

The big fellow turned and gave me a wide smile. "Why, hello, Mr. Courtney! Glad to see you. I just got in last night."

"And couldn't wait to get to work, I see."

Happy grinned self-consciously. He was a character, Happy. His last name was Kappel, and he was an old carnie from way back. He was the first to show up at the boardwalk every year and a kind of flunkey for Russo, who managed the walk for Moran. Happy had to be at least seventy, and he took little steps about five inches long. But he did more actual work than any of the other carnies on the lot.

I told Happy I was in a hurry and that I'd see him later. I didn't ask him if he'd seen Moran, for he was working for Moran, and would have just shaken his head. I figured Moran to be in the barber shop where he usually loafed.

He was there all right. Lew Cost, the barber, had him lathered up and was whetting his razor. Moran, staring at the ceiling, didn't see me, but when Lew said, "Hello, Perry," Moran had to say hello, too.

"I just pulled down a placard," I told Moran casually. "Seems your printer made a mistake. The thing says the Palace runs all season, seven nights a week."

"What's wrong about that?"

"Nothing, only it's running week-ends only. And since it seems the placard's the way you want it, would you mind telling me why you hired Hal Caldwell for the spot when I'm managing the place?"

"That's easy. Because you hired a band for only two nights, and that's not managing the Palace the way your contract reads."

"My contract doesn't say I'm to operate at a loss."

"You've got your salary, haven't you?"

"Salary, my eye! A lousy seventy a week can't cover a hundred loss! And that's what it'll be this year the way things are around here."

"Since when have you turned out to be such a prophet? I say we'll make money in the Palace this year. Anyway, it stays open every night, whether you like it or not."

I let it get me then. I went up to his chair and grabbed his coat front through the barber apron.

"Damn you, Moran, try and run the Palace every night and see what happens!"

Then I walked out before Moran could say a word. I hadn't taken fifty steps when I met Micky. She smiled and said hello, but I went right on by without saying a word. I knew it was a silly idea, even then, but I was so mad I kidded myself into thinking Micky had helped her father steer me into the Palace deal.

I DIDN'T cool off at all. I made the mistake of stopping in at Woody's place and was even dumb enough to tell Woody my story while he kept a shot glass full of whiskey in front of me. By the time it was dark I'd made up my mind to beat the hell out of Jim Moran.

I remembered I'd left my car parked in the boardwalk lot, not a good place to leave it even after the season opens, when the place gets some policing. I got it and drove in back of Moran's hotel. The back door was ajar this time and light showed through.

I walked right in.

"Hello," said Moran absently. He turned back to Hal Caldwell, who was standing across from Moran's desk. "Hal, I don't want any trouble with the local about union scale this year. Last year there were plenty of beefs. So long as I pay you good dough, I want you to pay scale."

Caldwell didn't like my being there. He looked embarrassed. He answered quickly. "O.K., Jim, think nothing of it. This year I got to pay scale or I don't get any sidemen. You needn't worry."

"Well. I hope I don't have to."

Caldwell got out fast. I looked after him and sneered.

"So that's your idea of a band leader? That jerk has no more business in front of a band than he has in front of the Third Army. He can't even read music. All he does is wave a stick while the drummer or somebody keeps the boys in time."

Moran said: "I don't care whether he can read music or not. The crowds like him. That's what pays off."

"Well, the crowds at the Palace aren't going to get a chance to like him. Caldwell's out. I've got a band for weekends, and that's the only time the joint runs this season."

"Now, Perry, let's not go into that again. The Palace opens next week for a straight season."

"The hell it does." I reached across Moran's desk and picked him up with both hands clutching his coat front. Then I let go with my right hand and swung for his jaw. I hit him so hard his coat lapels tore loose from my left hand, and he went over backwards in his chair. He got up swearing and came around the desk after me.

I was ready. I sank my right fist into his belly, and he grunted. Still he clipped me on the side of my face. It didn't hurt, it just made me madder. I really smeared him then, and he banged down on the floor, his head thrown back. It hit the corner of his safe. I knew from the sound that it was a bad deal. I bent over him at once, pulling his head away. Then I felt where it had hit the safe's edge, and it was a worse deal.

While I stared, he stopped breathing. I didn't know what to do. I had a hazy idea about getting a doctor, but I knew from the feel of the back of Moran's head, that even if he could be revived, he wouldn't last very long no matter how many doctors I got. I had no very clear idea of what crime I'd committed. I knew it wasn't murder, that it was manslaughter, perhaps. But I'd made a threat in the barber shop, and Lew Cost had overheard me. I thought there probably had been a couple other fellows waiting there, too.

But mostly I thought of Micky. She would never forgive me for this. No matter how much provocation Moran had given me, no matter how unintentional my killing him had been, she'd never speak to me again. My only out was to keep her from knowing.

I didn't even think twice. I spied a towel at the wash basin in the corner. I got it and wrapped it around Moran's head. There wasn't much blood. Moran was heavier than I had suspected, but it wasn't far to my car. Nobody else was in the lot, and nobody saw me stuff Moran in the back. Then I went back into the office to look things over.

There was a little blood on the linoleum floor near the safe. I got out my spare handkerchief and soaked it at the wash basin. Wiping up the blood was easy, but I'd read about how hard it was to remove all traces, so I rang out the handkerchief again and again, soaking it all over and washing the spot on the linoleum till I was sure there was no telltale trace.

Then I picked up Moran's chair and put it where it belonged behind his desk. I snapped out the lights and closed the door behind me, making sure the night lock was on. I got under the wheel of my car, turned around and headed for my place on the north side of the lake.

MORAN'S BOARDWALK is, of course, on the south side of Lake Prescott, and it's nine miles to my place. That meant nine miles of traveling on state highways and plenty of risk being picked up by the patrol. Any cop would have said I was drunk from looking at me and smelling my breath, but the fact is I'd completely sobered. I was thinking automatically, and, I think, pretty efficiently.

My plan was to weight Moran's body and dump him into the old and natural part of Prescott Lake. Mostly the lake is shallow, for it's an artificial one, but the original lake is about sixty feet deep. Nobody would find Moran there.

Weighting the body didn't bother me much, for the man who'd sold me my place had left a lot of rowboat anchors and chains. As I drove, I worked out how I was going to fasten them securely, and it didn't take me long after I got there. My place is pretty well isolated, and nobody bothered me at my work.

My thirty-foot cruiser stood ready in the boat house, but I didn't use it. I put Moran into my fourteen-foot fishing boat and started the kicker. People might notice the two-hundred-horse motor in the inboard, but plenty of fishermen were out with outboard motors. My only hope was they wouldn't happen along until I'd dumped my cargo in the old lake.

I got there without meeting a soul. Moran went over with a quiet splash, and I headed home. On the way back a fisherman crossed my path a few rods ahead, but I'm sure he couldn't have identified me even if he'd known me, which he probably didn't. All in all, the thing was pretty well carried off.

But I didn't sleep that night. Next day Micky called me and asked if I'd seen her dad, and I said no. She hung up without undue excitement, for Moran had left without notice on many a drunk before. Sometimes he was gone for a week and then would wire home for money from Chicago or Miami. Only this time he was getting ready to open the boardwalk, and Micky knew that with her dad it was always business before benders.

I couldn't bear to look at her at the end of the second day. She came over to the North Side to see me and cried like a baby. I patted her a while and tried to calm her, but it was no use. Suddenly she looked up and wanted to know why I hadn't spoken to her the time after I'd left Lew Cost's barber shop.

I told her frankly that I'd been upset over an argument with her father. Then she told me there was talk going around about that argument, and that Lew Cost was telling all his customers that I'd made a threat against her father right there in his shop.

"Of course I don't take any stock in it," said Micky, sniffling, "but I hate to have such talk going around. If Dad doesn't show up I think I'll go nuts."

I thought I would, too. I stuck it out another day, hiding once and pretending not to be at home when I saw Micky coming. She pounded the doors till I thought they'd come down, but I stayed put out of sight, unable to face her. After she'd left, I put on my coat and hat and drove into the city. I went directly to the sheriff's office and told the deputy in charge that I wanted to make a confession.

He got Harry Malone, the district attorney, and Malone came on the run with a stenographer. I then dictated this confession, which I hereby sign without any hope of reward or fear of threat, voluntarily under neither constraints nor duress.

(Signed: Perry Courtney)

(Witnessed by Lucille Green and Jane Stolle).

"And that, Your Honor," said Harry Malone, "is Perry Courtney's confession. I ask the Court that it be admitted as the State's Exhibit Number One."

"And I object," said Clarence Darrow Mort, rising.

MORT, ATTORNEY for the defendant, Perry Courtney, gave his client a reassuring wink before he addressed the judge, who eyed him with wary interest.

"On what grounds do you object to the introduction of the confession, Mr. Mort? It seems to be regular in form."

"I object," said Mort, "on the ground that the State has failed to prove a *corpus delicti*. In his confession Courtney said he put Moran's body in Prescott Lake. Well, where's the body? Outside the confession itself there's been no proof that there was a dead body!"

Malone turned a slightly sneering gaze on his adversary.

"Certainly so distinguished a criminal lawyer as you, Mr. Mort, wouldn't be so stupid as to think a *corpus delicti* is the body of the murdered man. It is the body of the crime. And that may be proved by circumstantial evidence, as any correspondence law course would tell you!"

Mort, a pygmy before the towering figure of the youthful district attorney, bowed humbly.

"My apologies, Mr. Malone. Owing to the paper shortage, my correspondence law lessons have been arriving a little late. But I seem to remember one about a confession being no proof of crime without some corroboration. If the judge's lessons have arrived on time, maybe he remembers the same thing."

"Gentlemen!" said the judge, hiding a grin behind his hand, "you must remember that you are officers of this court and entitled to mutual respect. I'll reserve opinion on defendant's objection while you proceed, Mr. Malone. You may offer such evidence in corroboration of the confession as you have."

Malone turned slightly pale.

"But Your Honor, I'm ready to rest my case once the confession is admitted! I've already corroborated it with the testimony of the barber. Lew Cost, and three of his customers, who were in his shop when Courtney threatened Moran. Also I've offered the testimony of the band leader, Hal Caldwell, who left Moran alone with Courtney. And then Miss Moran herself—"

"Your witnesses corroborated certain facts stated in the confession," interrupted Mort, "but not those facts pertaining to Moran's death or its cause. There is not one scintilla of evidence that Moran is dead—outside the confession itself!"

Malone wiped his brow, fairly soaking a handkerchief.

"But, Your Honor, Moran disappeared on the night when Courtney confessed that he killed him. No one has seen him since. Certainly that is corroboration of the confession!"

"It proves only that Moran has disappeared," said Mort. "Where's your proof that he is dead? That handkerchief in your hand reminds me of the handkerchief Moran mentioned in his confession, the one with which he washed the blood from the linoleum. Where is that handkerchief that would have tell-tale blood stains? Where's your expert evidence that blood was ever on that linoleum floor? That's the kind of evidence you need to corroborate the confession of Perry Courtney!"

Malone snorted. "You know well enough that we haven't been able to find the handkerchief and that the linoleum tests were negative! You also know that the bottom of the old lake is so tricky that when we dropped test bundles the size of a human body we couldn't find them."

Mort nodded. "All that I know, but I don't know that Jim Moran is dead!"

The judge cleared his throat.

"Mr. Malone, am I to understand that you have no further evidence?"

"Well, I—I—well, no, Your Honor. But—"

"Then the defendant's objection is sustained. It is my further order, *sua sponte,* that the jury retire to its room and return a verdict of not guilty!"

CHAPTER TWO

ENTER—THE CORPSE

IT TOOK a double-header in a back booth at Milligan's saloon to bring Perry Courtney out of his trance. Still dazed, he stared unbelievingly across the table at the lined face of his lawyer.

"But, Mr. Mort, I can hardly believe it! Do you mean I'm free and that I can never be tried again for Moran's death?"

"Of course. You cannot be placed in jeopardy twice for the same crime."

"Well, I just can't understand it. I confessed, didn't I? I'm the last one to complain, but it does seem to me that it's a crazy technicality that won't let a man be convicted of a crime, even when he's voluntarily signed a confession!"

Mort regarded his client thoughtfully. "Well, suppose you hadn't actually killed Moran?"

"But in that case why should I confess?"

"I'll bite. Why did you?"

Courtney started, then forced a laugh. "You can't be serious."

"But I am. I doubt that you killed Moran. You could have confessed to protect somebody else. There's the girl, Micky."

"Now that's plain nuts! You heard her testify against me and saw how she treated me in the courtroom. Why, she wouldn't even speak to me. Don't tell me she was acting—no actress is that good!"

"I'll admit her loathing seemed on the level. But you might have confessed thinking you were protecting her when actually she was as innocent as you. That would account for her attitude."

"You've got a wrong idea, Mr. Mort. Micky certainly didn't kill her father, and she had no reason to. I ought to know, because I did."

Mort shrugged. "That's your story, and you can stick to it as long as you like. It's no concern of mine who killed Moran or why. My job is done. Which reminds me that you owe me my fees."

"You don't have to remind me, Mr. Mort. You'll get your money, just as soon as Russo, the receiver, liquidates my interest. He's O.K. He'll sell to the highest bidder without any hanky-panky."

"I know Russo. That is, I used to know him pretty well. In fact, I did him a small favor once. I'm not worried about him, but I am worried about who's going to bid on the Palace. You're in no position to protect yourself. There's nothing to stop Micky Moran from stealing it for a song."

"Oh, yes there is. I've got a backer who'll enable me to protect my interests. Micky won't let me outbid her. I'll bid her up to fifty thousand and let her have it at that figure."

Mort turned an unimpressed gaze toward the bar and signaled the barman.

The barman brought another round. Then he looked up and said: "Sorry, lady, this place is strictly stag."

"But I've business here, and it'll only take a minute."

Courtney had risen from his seat and stood awkwardly in the booth. He reddened as he spoke to the blond girl standing at the table. "Micky! I didn't—"

"Sit down, Mr. Courtney. I've only this to say. In spite of Bob Martel's advice, I'm going to buy the Palace. I'll give you fifty thousand dollars. Exactly what you've put into it. You've taken out some profit. You should be satisfied. Is it a deal?"

"Why, of course, Micky, only—"

"Then have your lawyer in court tomorrow morning, and I'll pay off. All I ask is that you never show your face again at Prescott Lake."

She walked out. Courtney's face grew even redder after she had left. He eyed Mort with no attempt to cover his embarrassment.

"Well, that's that. You'll have your money as soon as she pays off. It was ten thousand, I believe."

"And no cents. You can leave the check with my secretary."

"It'll be a pleasure. You saved my life, and I'm grateful."

"That I doubt—I mean that I saved your life. I doubt even that Moran is dead."

"Wrong on that one, boss."

Both men looked up. The youth towering at the table was over six and a half feet tall.

MORT SMILED into Courtney's puzzled face. "I don't think you've met my junior partner, Blackie Jones. Blackie's been doing a little undercover work out at Prescott Lake— if you can imagine him keeping under cover. By the way, Blackie, just what did you mean by that crack?"

"Simply what I said. You're wrong about Moran not being dead. About twenty minutes ago a fisherman came in to the lake superintendent's office and said he'd found Moran's body. I tried to get you by phone at the court house, but you'd left."

Courtney was white.

"You—you're kidding!"

"No, I'm not kidding. Moran was floating top-side up, and there was a tattoo mark on his chest. The fish had eaten away a lot of his flesh, but not the tattoo mark. You probably remember such a mark, Mr. Courtney."

"A four-masted schooner in green and red?"

"Right. The—"

Courtney was out of the booth and past Blackie Jones. He did not bother to grab his hat from its hook as he raced from Milligan's.

"Sit down, Blackie," said Mort quietly, "and tell me all about it."

Blackie Jones was able to get into the booth only because Courtney in his haste had pushed back the table. He put his huge elbows on its surface and gave Mort a dour smile.

"I was only obeying instructions. Ever since the trial began I've been parking at the State Conservation office at Prescott Lake. It's got so the lake superintendent and conservation officers are tired of looking at me. They couldn't figure out why I was there. Neither could I. Don't tell me you knew the body was going to be found!"

"I won't. But I considered the possibility that it would. If it were found, I wanted to be the first to know about it."

"I see. You'd have had Courtney take a plea in that case."

"Exactly. Malone was so leery of his case that he'd have settled for manslaughter."

"He had a right to be leery. What I can't figure out is why he ever brought it to trial anyway. He knew he couldn't prove a *corpus delicti*."

"Public pressure, my lad. Courtney confessed to Moran's murder three months ago. The public demanded a trial. Malone had been running in luck, winning a few tough cases, and he figured that a jury would convict Courtney on the confession alone. He was probably right. That's why I had to stop that confession from ever going to the jury. It seems I did it in the nick of time."

"It couldn't have been much closer. I wonder why the body didn't turn up before."

"That's easy. The murderer planted it in some other part of the lake. Then it was redeposited in the old lake proper with the chains taken off so that inevitably it would rise to the surface. The party who planted it this second time mistakenly thought the trial would last several more days and the case against Courtney would be cinched by its discovery."

Blackie Jones frowned in perplexity. "You're way ahead of me. Am I to understand that Courtney lied in his confession about where he placed the body and that later someone else found it and dropped it where it was supposed to be?"

"You're to understand that Courtney lied in his confession. But not that he planted the body somewhere else. He never planted it anywhere, because he never murdered Moran. The murderer put the body in the lake on the night when Courtney said he killed Moran, but not until later—last night probably—did he put the body where it was found this afternoon."

"But how can you know all that? How can you be so sure Courtney didn't kill Moran? What makes you believe someone was trying to frame him at the last minute?"

"I know Courtney didn't kill Moran because of the way he acted when you came in here and announced that Moran's body had been found. His reaction was one of dumfounded incredulity. I'd had my doubts before, but then I knew. Knowing Courtney didn't kill Moran, it's easy to figure that someone else was trying to take advantage of his confession and frame him for keeps."

"But if Courtney didn't murder Moran, why did he confess?"

"To protect somebody, of course."

"You mean the daughter, Micky?"

"No. She thinks Courtney's guilty."

"Then who?"

"When I find that out I'll know who the murderer is. Right now I've only the vaguest idea."

"Then what's your vague idea?"

"It's too vague, Blackie. I won't commit myself until I've some proof."

"You mean to get some?"

"Sure."

"Why? Your job of defending Courtney's over, isn't it?"

"Before a jury, yes, but not before the world. Now that the body's been found, everybody will think that Courtney's guilty and that he actually killed Moran. He needs me now more than he ever did before. I don't intend to let him down."

"Well, that's the first time I ever heard of you working for the same fee twice."

"I'm not so sure I've earned it once yet."

"I don't follow you."

"You will. Come, let's get out of here. We're driving out to Prescott Lake. If Courtney hadn't been so precipitous, we'd all have gone out together."

Mort looked tiny beside his gigantic junior partner as they drove out to Prescott Lake. Half an hour later they pulled up at the State Conservation office. A crowd was milling around the small frame building situated on piling and bordered by wooden docks on the two sides adjacent to the lake. Conservation officers were keeping back the crowds. Mort permitted Blackie Jones to make way through the crowd, which fell back with alacrity at the giant's approach.

"I want to see the superintendent," Mort announced to an officer. "I'm attorney for Perry Courtney."

The officer gave him a look of recognition and he was permitted to pass through. Jones followed, and the officer made no attempt to stop him, saying only: "You back? I thought we'd got rid of you finally!"

The pair skirted the end of the conservation office and reached the little group on the far side. The group consisted of Phil Sutton, the conservation superintendent, Dr. Reynolds, the county coroner, and Harry Malone. Malone looked up angrily.

"Well, Mort, I hope you're satisfied! You wanted proof of a *corpus delicti*. Take a look at this!"

Mort looked, then looked away quickly. He heard Blackie Jones gag behind him.

More to cover up his reaction than anything else, Mort asked: "The fisherman who found him, where's he?"

"In my office," said Sutton. "This thing's made him about half sick."

Mort nodded to Blackie Jones, and they retreated into the office. A man in fishing togs sat with elbows on knees. He lifted a sallow face as the two men entered. Mort eyed him with respectful curiosity.

"You found the body?"

"I sure did. It sure fixed up my vacation. Brother, was that a sight!"

He shook his head. Mort glanced toward Blackie Jones.

"I'm C.D. Mort, the criminal lawyer defending Perry Courtney. This is Blackie Jones, my partner. Any information you can give us about the discovery of the body will be highly appreciated."

The man shrugged. "My name's Wright, Dave Wright. I've just been here a couple of days of what was to be two weeks' vacation. The way I feel now, I want to pack my bags and go home."

"You came here alone?"

"No. Three other fellows along. We've been fishing together for two days and ain't caught nothing and today I said: 'Boys, you go your way, and I'll go mine. I think you bring me bad luck.' Bad luck! Wow! If only I'd stayed with them! I didn't know what bad luck was!"

"Do you recall exactly when you first noticed the body?"

"Pretty near. At first I didn't think nothing of it, just thought it was a submerged log floating. Then I moved over a little closer, thinking there might be some fish around a log. When I got closer I saw it wasn't no log."

"And what time was that?"

"Four o'clock. When I saw it was a body I knew it'd be important to check the time, so I checked. It was only about a minute after four."

"What did you do then?"

"I started my kicker and beat it in here to the conservation office. I told the superintendent what I'd found. Then he got the big boat and one of the officers, and we all went out. He was plenty excited, because he said right away it was Jim Moran's body. Especially after I told him about seeing the tattoo."

"Oh, you saw that, did you?"

"Sure. The body was practically under water but chest up."

Mort turned to Blackie Jones. "That right?"

"That's right. That's the way it happened. I left immediately."

Again Mort faced the fisherman. "How long did it take you to get here from where you found the body?"

"About twenty minutes I'd say."

"Let me see, aren't there some cottages pretty close to the deep part of Prescott Lake, only a few hundred yards away?"

"Yes, I guess it's not much farther than that."

"Yet you came clear to this place instead of landing near one of the cottages and phoning?"

"Well, I'm a stranger around here. I didn't suppose any of them cottages had phones. The cottage us fellows got hasn't."

MORT EYED Blackie Jones. "Well, one thing is definite. The body wasn't found until after the judge had ruled out the confession and directed a verdict of acquittal. You tried to get me at the court house the moment after Wright arrived here with the news of finding the body, didn't you?"

"Almost the same moment. The superintendent grabbed the phone and called the coroner, then I tried to get you. They said you'd just left and that Courtney had been freed. The matter no longer seemed so urgent, so I gave up trying to reach you by phone and drove in."

"Well, allowing for five minutes for the superintendent to get the coroner, that makes twenty-five minutes between the time when Wright found the body and the time when you tried to get me. I was forty minutes getting a journal entry typed and approved by Harry Malone after the jury returned its directed verdict. So the body wasn't found until fifteen minutes after Courtney was in the clear."

Blackie Jones shrugged. "Well, it was close enough at that. By the way, where is Courtney? I thought you said he left Milligan's in such a hurry because he couldn't believe Moran was dead. If he really didn't think Moran was dead, wouldn't he want to find out for sure? I'd think that'd be the first thing he'd do."

"So do I." Mort looked up as Malone and the superintendent entered. "Has Courtney been here yet?"

The superintendent shook his head.

Malone grimaced. "You didn't really expect him to come here, did you? This is the last place he'd want to come!"

The superintendent eyed Blackie Jones a little resentfully. "So you're Mort's new law partner, are you? And here I thought all along that you wanted to write up Prescott Lake for a magazine!"

"That shows clear enough you knew Moran's body was in the lake," accused Malone. "If you hadn't known, you wouldn't have planted Jones out here to keep tabs."

Mort shrugged. "You're sure that *is* Moran's body, are you?"

"Of course. Everybody around the lake can identify that tattoo mark, even if the fish did eat away his face."

Malone started then, for a muffled cry had sounded behind him. Everyone eyed Micky Moran. White-faced, she stood in the doorway. Plainly she had heard the district attorney's remark.

"I—I've just heard," she said. "Where is he?"

"He's back of the building," said the superintendent. "But you mustn't look. It wouldn't do any good."

The girl started to go anyway, but after one step she halted. Then she turned away from the rear of the building and moved out toward the curious crowd.

"Well," said Mort, "we can't do any good here either. Let's go, Blackie."

Beyond the fringe of the mob, Mort said: "Blackie, you need a shave."

"But I don't! Why, I had a shave at noon!"

"I said you need a shave. There's a barber in town named Lew Cost. His shop should be full at this time, but the longer you have to wait, the better. Pick up all the local talk about this thing that you can. I'm going to contact Russo out at the boardwalk. Call me there at his office."

"I don't much like this," Blackie Jones growled. "First you make me sit out the trial at Prescott Lake. Now you want me to have a scraped face!" But he trudged off in the direction of the Cost barber shop.

CHAPTER THREE
BARBER SHOP CHORUS

MORT WENT toward the boardwalk on the far side of the bay. It was a time in the late afternoon when a lull had struck. Hardly a soul was visible on the walk, and the concession operators loafed in pairs, every other concession unmanned. Mort broke up one conversation.

"I'm looking for Russo, the park manager. Know where I can find him?"

"The office," was the reply. "That's down the middle of the walk to the right."

Mort moved on. He stopped short when a voice cooed: "Try your luck, mister? It'll cost you a dime."

Mort smiled at the girl lounging on her elbows over the concession counter. She was blond and curvaceous. Her dress was cut low, and her lounging position made the effect terrific.

"Do I look as if I came from the country?" Mort asked. "Don't tell me you can't make that raffle wheel sit up and talk!"

The girl grinned goodhumoredly.

"So you think I'm not on the level, huh? Well, just to show you I've got a square deal, I'll give you a number. See, I'm putting this dime for you on twenty-six. Now, try your luck on me!"

The blonde spun the wheel. After some seconds it slowed and finally stopped on No. 26. The girl yipped with delight.

"See, you must be lucky! You've won two dollars, and it hasn't cost you a dime!"

She put two one-dollar bills on the counter.

Mort came closer. "You're actually giving me two dollars?"

"Sure! You won, didn't you? Help yourself!"

Mort laughed self-consciously. "Oh, I couldn't do that. Tell you what, let them ride on twenty-six."

"O.K., Lucky!" The girl put the bills on No. 26 and again spun the wheel. It stopped on No. 15.

"Eek! That's too bad!" The girl looked genuinely distressed. "Tell you what, cover up the two dollars, and it'll still ride."

"I don't get it. I lost, didn't I?"

"Oh, it's a rule of the game. You can always protect your losses if you double up."

Mort reached into his pocket and produced a roll of bills. He found two one's and placed them beside those already on the number.

Again the girl spun the wheel. Mort noted that it had thirty numbers. This time it stopped on No. 25.

"Boy, that was close," said the blonde. "Why don't you cover up again? This time it'll cost you four dollars, but if you win, you win a hundred and sixty. Want to try it?"

She had a doubtful look in her eye, so Mort threw down a five and picked up a dollar in change. The girl was about to spin the wheel when Mort heard a snicker behind him.

"Well, well! So the famous legal-light falls for a pitch-man's patter!"

Mort turned. A sleek, black-haired man of medium build smilingly extended his hand. Mort shook it.

"Hello, Russo. I was on my way to see you."

"But you got side-tracked, didn't you? Of all people! I never thought you'd fall for a variation of the 'Capital Prize' game! If I hadn't come along Winnie'd had you hooked for half a bill before you knew what the score was!"

"Say, what is the score?" yipped the blonde. "What's the idea, Russo, gummin' my pitch?"

"Shiazut yiazour liazip," said Russo. "Thiazis giazuy's iaza piazal iazof miazine!"

"Well, why didn't you say so?" said the blonde. She sorted out the money and gave Mort back his investment.

"Are my ears deceiving me?" asked Mort, picking up the money, "or were you talking in some hitherto unknown language? I used to fancy myself something of a linguist, but that's a new one."

Russo grinned. "It's an unknown language outside the carnival world. I'll explain it to you sometime."

MORT REGARDED the blonde. "Suppose you explain right now how this charming lady exercises such control over that wheel, making it stop at whatever number she wants it to. Believe me, she hadn't taken me in—I was only trying to see if I could catch her working a brake."

The blonde grinned derisively.

Russo laughed. "Now you've insulted her. Only an amateur would use a brake to stop a wheel. It's too crude. Even the round haircuts get wise when the wheel stops too sudden."

"Then how does she stop it?"

"She backs it up."

"I don't get it."

"Back it up for him, Winnie, and stop on Fifteen."

The girl grasped the wheel with her index finger at the back of the rim, backed it up slightly and spun it forward. It stopped on No. 15.

Russo grinned. "Get it now?" Mort shook his head. Russo shrugged. "Do it again, Winnie. This time stop it on Twenty."

The girl again seized the wheel, backed it up a little farther, and it stopped on No. 20. Mort's expression was still blank. Russo regarded him as if he were a backward child.

"It's like this: Winnie backs up the wheel before she spins it. The distance she backs it up depends on what number she wants. The idea is she spins it the same way every time, and it always turns the same number of revolutions. The way she gets different numbers is putting her finger in a different slot in the back of a wheel. For Fifteen she puts it in one slot. For another number, she puts it in another. The wheel always spins the same way. Now do you get it?"

"I don't know. Are you implying that she spins the wheel so accurately that it always spins the same number of times before it stops?"

"Oh, Winnie may miss once in a hundred times. But then she's a youngster at the game."

Winnie frowned. "The hell I miss! You just come around and watch. I'll work free every week I miss just that first time!"

Russo laughed. "Come on Mort, you wanted to see me. I suppose about Moran. I wish I could congratulate you for winning your case, but I can't. After all, Moran was my boss, and I'm working for his girl now."

"You saw the body?"

"Sure. I was one of the first to identify it."

"Then you're sure it's Moran?"

"Absolutely. There'd never be two guys walking around here with that schooner on their chests. And what's left of him indicates a man about Moran's height. But suppose we go to my office and talk."

"Sure." Mort paused long enough to toss back the money the girl had returned to him. "Keep it," he said. "The demonstration alone was worth it, not to mention the opportunity to talk to a creature as lovely as yourself."

The girl beamed, almost blushed. "Gee, thanks, mister! I think you're kind of cute yourself!"

RUSSO LAUGHED loudly as he moved away with Mort. "Better look into that, Mr. Mort. Winnie's a nice kid. Don't get any wrong ideas because she takes the marks with a wheel. That's the only business these carnies know. They grow up in it, and it's just as legit to them as banking."

"And much more profitable," said Mort. "I never dreamed Moran had such a layout here. No wonder he wanted to keep the Palace open as a feeder for all these concessions."

"Yes, it's a shame he didn't buy young Courtney out at a nice profit. Then there wouldn't have been any trouble. I advised him to do that, but he wouldn't."

"You seem to have been pretty close to Moran. Know much about his background?"

"No. I've worked for him for five years. All I know is he came here ten years ago and built up this place from practically nothing. I suppose you know that it was appraised at three hundred grand."

"Yes, it was a nice estate for Bob Martel to settle—and for the girl to keep, since she was the only beneficiary in the will."

"Of course. A grand kid, Micky. I'm glad you didn't come around here questioning me before the trial. I'd have hated to turn you down, despite the favor you once did for me. But I couldn't have done anything that Micky wouldn't have wanted."

"Kinda like her, don't you?"

"Skip it, Mr. Mort. You know my background. I wouldn't do that to her."

Mort shrugged.

They entered the carnival manager's office and Russo got out a bottle. They both had liberal drinks. Then Russo eyed Mort quizzically across his desk.

"What I wanted to see you about is this band leader, Caldwell. He was in the hotel office the night Moran disappeared. Courtney seemed to think that as a band leader he was no good. If that was true, why would Moran have hired him? Moran was a showman."

Russo shook his head. "You got me there, Mr. Mort. I had to agree with Courtney about Caldwell. His music stinks. He was lousy even for the night club, and I couldn't figure it at all when Moran put him in the Palace."

"He's still there, isn't he? You're the receiver, why don't you throw him out?"

"Because he's got an air-tight contract. It's a union form, only the two-weeks clause is stricken out. I'm stuck with Caldwell for the rest of the season."

Mort frowned thoughtfully.

The phone rang and Russo picked up the cradle set and answered. He handed it to Mort.

Blackie Jones' voice came over the wire. "I'm calling from the barber shop. You were right when you said this place would be a hotbed for gossip. I've got something really hot. The local talk is our client Courtney's pulled a fast one all the way around. He's supposed to have collected fifty grand for his interest in the Palace, then killed Moran and pocketed the receipt. His idea was to collect again from Moran's estate, after he beat the murder rap. Seems he had an idea he couldn't be fried so long as a body wasn't found."

Mort said impatiently: "I'm disappointed in you, Blackie. You should recognize barbershop bull. Call me back when you've got something that's the McCoy."

"O.K. Only you might be interested to know that the guy doing the talking was Bob Martel, Moran's lawyer. He's still in the chair all lathered up so he can't see who's in the shop. He says he's not going to let Micky pay off tomorrow."

"I still won't buy. Without a receipt he can't prove a thing."

"The hell he can't. Moran withdrew fifty thousand from his checking account the day he was killed. Maybe you recall that in the inventory of the estate there was practically no cash. What's more, the bank kept a record of the numbers on those bills. Martel's showing around a list to prove it!"

Mort whistled softly. "That's enough. Pick me up here at Russo's office. We're going to have a little talk with Courtney."

CHAPTER FOUR
TATTOO FOR TWO

DRIVING AWAY from the parking lot Blackie Jones asked: "Where do you expect to find him? Could be he's taken it on the lam. If so, good-by our fees."

Mort shrugged. "We'll try his cottage on the north side. There's no phone, we'll have to drive. It's at least ten miles, so step on it."

They made it in less than fifteen minutes. Blackie Jones shot a look at Mort as he turned into Courtney's drive. Courtney's car was parked beside his cottage. Both car doors slammed together as the pair left the car. Mort tried the side door and got no answer. He nodded, and Blackie Jones went around in front. A moment later he returned with a shrug. He followed Mort to the rear door. It was ajar. Mort knocked, yelled when he got no answer. He entered the cottage, and Blackie followed.

The kitchen was deserted. It, like the room beyond, had the stagnant air of an unused dwelling. The room beyond was the living room, for, like nearly all cottages at Prescott Lake, it was without a dining room. Bedrooms were located at one side. Mort entered one while Blackie Jones prowled the other. They met in the bath between.

For a moment neither spoke. Then Blackie Jones said: "Well, this time we've got a *corpus delicti!*"

Mort nodded wryly. Perry Courtney lay in his own bathtub, his head back against the faucet. He was stripped to shorts. A clotted stream of blood was drying on his chest. It was surmounted by a neat bullet hole. The hole was very near Courtney's heart.

His whitened fingers still clutched an automatic pistol. The weapon was held backwards in his right hand, so that the thumb, used as a trigger finger, squeezed away from his body. Blackie Jones winced as Mort bent and pried at the thumb. It would not budge. It gripped the trigger like a vise.

Mort shifted his gaze to the opposite side of the bath. Almost at once they found what they sought. Mort crossed the room and picked up the brass cartridge case. He inspected it briefly, tossed it back to its original position.

"Remington," he said. "A thirty-two automatic."

Blackie Jones nodded. "It's about where it should be. Looks like an authentic suicide, all right. Besides, suicides always like to take the clothes off whatever part of their body they're going to shoot. That's what Courtney did. He didn't even want to shoot through his undershirt, so he stripped to his shorts. He got into his bathtub besides. Well, he made a neat job of it. I'll say that for him."

Mort eyed him noncommittally. "And the motive?"

"Remorse, of course. So long as Moran's body didn't turn up, he could still look the world in the eye and say: 'You can't prove I killed Moran! Even though I lost my head and confessed, no body ever turned up.' But when the fisherman found Moran, he knew his game was up. That's why he left Milligan's in such a hurry. He couldn't wait to get it over with!"

Mort shrugged. "Well, I've been wrong before. But I'm sticking to my guns. Courtney didn't kill Moran. If he had thought Moran was dead, he never would have signed a confession. If the worst came to the worst, he counted on Moran coming forth to save his skin."

"But why would he do a thing like that? Why would he confess to killing Moran if Moran were still alive?"

"That's what I came here to ask Courtney. But somebody didn't want him to answer the sixty-four-dollar question. Somebody beat us here."

"You're only guessing. The clamped fingers around the gun prove that Courtney fired the fatal shot. And I bet a nitrate test will corroborate that."

"Neither proves a thing. Courtney could have been stunned. While still half-dazed his murderer could have put the pistol in his hand and forced his thumb to squeeze the trigger. That would account for the vise-like grip and any nitrate found on his hand. It still could be murder."

"All right, what are you going to do about it?"

"Find the murderer. I told you I was going to acquit Courtney in the eyes of the world, and I meant it. Finding the murderer and getting his confession—the real confession—is the only way to do it."

"Well, that's a large order. How do you propose to go about it?"

"The first thing is to find out what happened to the fifty thousand Moran drew from the bank the day he disappeared. If I had known about that, I might have had the key to this thing long ago."

"I wonder why Harry Malone didn't bring it out at the trial. He must have known about it."

"Of course he did. But if he had introduced that fact in evidence, a jury might have wondered if Moran hadn't meant to settle his trouble with Courtney all along. And if he had been in an appeasing mood, there wouldn't have been any trouble between the two men. So Malone was afraid Courtney would repudiate the confession and admit that he'd been paid off. He was afraid the truth would hurt his case."

"But you don't think Courtney was paid off?"

"No."

"Then who got the fifty thousand?"

"The man who killed Moran. The man who killed Courtney. There's fifty thousand clues to him, fifty thousand dollars. We've got to find their trail."

"If you don't mind my suggesting it, it'd do no harm to get out of here. I don't think we're very popular with Mr. Malone."

"No, we're not. But even Malone isn't dumb enough to think we murdered Courtney for our fees. You stay here, Blackie, while I drive to the nearest phone and report this thing. Don't expect me back. You can get a ride with somebody."

"I'm getting a ride right now! First I sit out Courtney's trial, then I sit it out with his corpse! What the hell!"

Mort chuckled. "Well, you'll have plenty of time to tell your troubles to Courtney!"

MORT STOPPED at the first cross-roads filling station and put in a call to the *Daily Banner,* a morning paper. Gail Collins, the city editor, was already on the job. Mort succinctly described the discovery of Courtney's body.

"You can quote me as saying that I have positive proof that it was murder."

"All right, what've you got?"

"You can also quote me as saying that I am not ready to divulge my positive proof."

Mort hung up. He called the sheriff's office. Henney Fielding, the sheriff, had perhaps never given him a break, but at least he hadn't gone out of his way to make trouble as Harry Malone had. Mort simply told Fielding that Courtney was dead and where the body could be found. He hung up again and drove directly to the Moran bungalow at Prescott Village.

It was a modest dwelling, looking coolly comfortable with a screened-in veranda. Mort parked in the drive and walked up the flagstone walk. He heard Micky Moran before he saw her.

She was sobbing as if her heart would break. She lay on a wicker lounge, face downward. Mort coughed. The girl straightened and eyed him angrily.

"What do you want here? Go away!"

Mort opened the screen door and stepped inside. He sat down in a wicker chair and surveyed the girl. She sat up, putting her feet on the floor. Her rage was almost beyond control.

"Perry Courtney is dead. Murdered."

The rage left the girl's face.

"Wh—where?"

"His cottage. We just found him, Blackie Jones and I."

"You say he was murdered? How do you know that?"

"The circumstances point to it. You can believe me—he was."

"But why? Who could have done it?"

"The same man who murdered your father."

"But Perry—"

"He didn't do it. True, he signed a confession, but he was the most astonished man in the world when he was told that your father was dead. Don't ask me what game he was playing, signing a phony confession—I don't know. But I do know that he's been murdered. Probably because he was the one person who could guess who actually planted that body in the lake."

Micky Moran wiped away the remnants of her tears. "But the district attorney, Mr. Malone, he—"

"He only wanted a conviction. That's why he wouldn't let you tell about the fifty thousand dollars your father drew from the bank the day he disappeared. Right?"

Micky's eyes widened. "Who told you about that?"

"It's all over Prescott by now I suppose, for Bob Martel was spouting off in the barber shop. The theory was that your father withdrew the money to pay off Courtney for his interest in the Palace. I suppose you agreed with him."

"Yes. I did. But there was no receipt—we had no proof. I was going to pay Perry again just to get rid of him."

"Well, you're rid of him now. Haven't you any clue as to what your father did with the money?"

"Absolutely none. He wrote out a check to cash and took the money in thousand-dollar bills. None of them ever turned up. It just about wiped out his account, for he'd bought a lot of liquor for the club and hotel bars. It left me almost broke to open the season. Why, if Russo hadn't—"

"Yes?"

"Well, Russo advanced some payroll money."

"How much payroll money?"

"I don't think that's any of your business. But it was five thousand dollars."

Mort whistled. "Russo's come up in the world!"

"Well, he saves his money. And he gets a good salary. You aren't—"

"No, I'm just considering all angles. Russo could have got that fifty thousand as well as anyone else."

"You don't think Dad was killed for the money?"

"No. But I think the murderer has the money. It's about the only lead I've got."

"But surely the authorities—"

"The authorities will—"

"Will prove you're a liar!" said a voice at the screen door.

Mort frowned. "Hello, Bob. Just what do you mean by that crack?"

"I mean Perry Courtney wasn't murdered. You made that up out of whole cloth."

Bob Martel opened the door and came inside. He was the bright young type, the modern lawyer who wears the bench-made clothes and an alert, go-get-'em expression. He eyed Mort as if he were an anachronistic curiosity.

"It's no use, Mort. Harry Malone landed at Courtney's cottage a few minutes after you left. He called me right after he called the coroner. There's no doubt as to what the coroner's verdict will be." Martel faced Micky. "Courtney's a suicide. When your father's body was found, he couldn't take it. He shot himself with an automatic in his own bathroom. It's open and shut."

The stunned girl's eyes lost their bewilderment. She whirled on Mort.

"Get out! Get out!"

Mort shrugged and left the veranda.

WHEN HE drove back to the boardwalk nearly every booth was closed, for it was dinner time. He found Russo's office locked. A man at a ring game told him Russo had left, that he lived at the hotel and that meant he was off the lot. Mort gave up and drove back to the city.

He went directly to his office building. It was already locked, but the night man let him in.

"A girl tried to get in here, but I wouldn't let her. I didn't like her looks. She was too showy."

"Blonde or brunette?"

"Blonde."

"Did she have a lot of—uh—"

"She sure did!"

"If she comes back, let her in. I'll wait for her."

"Sure, Mr. Mort. I guess I did wrong. I didn't know she—"

"That's O.K., Pop. You did exactly right. Only this is an exceptional case."

He rode the elevator to his floor, keyed himself into his private office. Winnie, the girl from the concession, sat in his swivel chair with her bare legs propped on his desk. She smiled.

"Hello. Mr. Mort."

"How did you get in here? Pop said—"

"He's a dear, isn't he? But he's not too bright. Joey, the guy who drove me in, only had to fall down once to get the old dear away from his door. He rushed out like the Good Samaritan he is, and I beat it inside."

"The lock on my door. You come through the keyhole?"

"With a hairpin. But don't bother to change your lock. I could open the First National just as easy."

"Remind me to draw out my money and put it in the Second National. You must have had something important on your mind, breaking and entering like this."

"I was only trying to help. I've got something to tell you."

"It can wait. You like rye or bourbon?"

"Scotch."

"Water or soda?"

"Don't tell me you've got the mixer right here in your office?"

A little smugly, Mort rounded his desk, stooped and opened a bottom drawer, observing that there was nothing lacking in his visitor's leg department. She, in turn, was genuinely appreciative as she regarded the opened drawer.

"Why, you've got a refrigerator built right in! You're a genius!"

Very smugly now, Mort poured soda and dropped in two cubes. From another drawer he withdrew two bottles. From one he poured a liberal portion of Scotch into the glass. From the other, bourbon into a double-jigger. He stirred the Scotch and soda with a lead pencil and passed it over.

"Here's to you, Winnie. I hope your story's a good one."

"It will be. But aren't you going to get a chaser?"

"And ruin my stomach? Bottoms up, child!"

Elbows bent in unison. Mort put down his jigger with ineffable satisfaction.

"First today. Now, what was it you were saying…"

"I think I've really got something, Mr. Mort. I've been thinking real hard about it ever since the body was found this afternoon. Then you came along, and you were so cute."

"Well, thanks. You mean the few dollars I tossed you were cute."

"It's not like that at all, Mr. Mort. I thought you were just real nice anyway. Of course it didn't hurt any when you passed back that dough after Russo queered my pitch. Just let him try to make me turn that in! It was a tip, wasn't it?"

"Sure. Now, this tip of yours—"

"Well, everybody's saying the body had to be Jim Moran's because he was the only guy who had a boat tattooed on his chest just like that one. Well, I happen to know different."

"Do you, indeed! Let these old ears have it before apoplexy hits me! Who else besides Moran wore that tattoo?"

"You wouldn't know him. He's an old carnie who's been around the boardwalk every season for years. Happy Kappel. Only this year he disappeared the same night Jim Moran did!"

"This Happy, he the same general size as Moran?"

"They could have passed as twins so far as build was concerned. I never thought about it until this afternoon, because they were so different every other way. Moran was a big-shot while poor old Happy just puttered around for three squares and a place to flop back of one of the games."

"How come nobody else remarked that both men wore identical tattoos?"

"I don't think anyone knew. I happened to find out because one evening last year I felt sorry for Happy and took him a quarter of a cake I'd baked. The door was open because it was plenty hot, and I just walked in. Happy was there in his shorts. I laughed till the tears came at the way he rushed around covering up. You'd think he was some old maid!"

"Did he cover up his chest first?"

"He did. Then he pulled on his pants, all the time begging me to get out. I would have only I couldn't, I was laughing so hard. It never occurred to me that he was trying to hide that tattoo, though, come to think of it, in even the hottest weather he wore his shirt buttoned up. Jim Moran used to go around with half his chest exposed. He was the boss, and he did what he pleased."

"And no one's seen Happy since Moran disappeared?"

"No one!"

Mort slapped his forehead with the palm of his hand.

"Ye Gods, senile dementia must be setting in! Courtney mentioned Happy Kappel in his confession. Kappel was on the boardwalk when he was looking for Moran!

I wondered why Harry Malone never turned him up as a witness, but I thought nothing of it, for Happy would only corroborate the confession anyway. I didn't bother to look him up, for Malone had all the other witnesses sewed up so tight I couldn't get a peep out of them. But I might have figured Malone would have rung in Happy, if only he'd known where to find him!"

"Perhaps he never thought of looking in Prescott Lake."

MORT SAID nothing to that. He smiled noncommittally and mixed her another drink, pouring one for himself. She actually trembled when she accepted hers.

"You think then I've brought you something important?"

"Important! You've brought the missing piece of this jig-saw that'll enable me to put the rest of it together! Why, I—"

Mort turned. The outside door had opened. He waited. Presently Blackie Jones entered. Mort nodded.

"Winnie, meet Blackie. He's my partner."

"Boy! What a hunk of man! Say, fellow, if it's not too personal, why aren't you in the Army?"

Blackie Jones scowled, but not too severely. There was something about Winnie's propped-up legs that cushioned her bluntness.

Mort explained quickly: "Blackie's an inch too tall for the Army. He tried every way to get in, even scrooching his head down between his shoulders. But they stopped him. The Army can't bother with exceptional cases like Blackie."

"Blackie? Why a nickname like that when his hair's blond? And natural, I can see, not peroxide like mine!"

Again Mort volunteered the information, as Blackie Jones winced painfully.

"It's like this, Winnie. Blackie's real name is Blackstone, after William Blackstone, the eighteenth-century commentator on the law. He just doesn't like to be kidded about it. So he hides under a pseudonym."

Blackie Jones scowled. "Since we're going in for revelations, did you happen to know that Mort's initials, C.D., stand for Clarence Darrow? He's touchy about it because he keeps pretending that he became a criminal lawyer only through the coincidence of the name. He also pretends that he hates the practice of law. Of course nothing could be farther from the truth. He couldn't be the top criminal lawyer of the country if he didn't like what he was doing."

Winnie eyed Mort with new interest. "Why, I'd think you'd be proud, Mr. Mort, of toting around such a distinguished name!"

Mort shot a murderous look at Blackie Jones. "Indeed I am, Winnie, only my real reason for not using it is that I'm not worthy of it. Darrow was more than a great criminal lawyer. He was one of the most enlightened men of his time. He fought trials for humanity while I fight mine for money. He—"

"Listen to him!" scoffed Blackie Jones. "He's batting his brain out right now trying to clear the name of a dead man! What kind of money does he get out of that? Do you think Courtney's heirs will appreciate it?"

Mort looked pained. "Since you've brought the subject around to my late client, what's new? Did the sheriff arrive?"

"Not until after Harry Malone happened along and took over with a brass band. You'll play the devil selling anything but a suicide theory to Malone. He's convinced Courtney's death merely proves him guilty beyond a reasonable doubt."

"So I've heard. I do hope the sheriff will exert enough pressure on the coroner to get a thorough investigation of the body. My guess is he'll find bruises if he looks close enough."

Blackie Jones shrugged. "I think you're crazy. If Courtney had been knocked out when he was shot, his fingers wouldn't have been clamped on the gun. They'd have been limp."

"That bothers me, but not much. I smell murder—the odor is unmistakable."

"My bet's on you," said Winnie, confidently. "Come on, Blackie, and have a drink. There's everything and plenty of it."

Blackie Jones regarded her dourly, but not with too much distaste. Mort grinned. "My brilliant young partner never touches the stuff. When tempted, he just thinks of me!"

Blackie Jones scowled. "Pay no attention to C.D. He thinks it's a joke because he's smarter lit than I am sober. But think how smart he'd be if he'd just lay off the stuff!"

Winnie shook her head. "I just wouldn't want to know anybody that smart!" She unpropped her legs, got up and stretched. "Well, boys, I've got to scram. The scatter I run opened a half hour ago, and Russo will skin me alive if I don't show pretty soon."

"And you have such lovely skin!" said Mort. "I'll buy another drink before you go."

Blackie Jones seemed to turn his back mentally as more whiskey was consumed.

Winnie had reached the door when Mort asked casually: "You're sure nobody else knew about the identical tattoo?"

"Absolutely—now wait! I told a lot of people about the way Happy had been embarrassed, but I never mentioned the tattoo to anybody but one person. Let me see."

Mort leaned forward. "Yes? Yes?"

"Now I remember! Hal Caldwell! That punk band leader. He was playing at the club then!"

She opened the door and vanished into the corridor.

CHAPTER FIVE
A MARK WITH A BEEF

FOR A moment both Mort and Blackie stared at the closed door. Then Blackie Jones said: "Well, what do you think?"

"I think I need to consult a brain specialist. So far I've been muddling through this case like a baby lost in the woods. My only excuse is that all I was trying to do was get an acquittal for Courtney. I knew I could do that without getting to the bottom of the mystery as to why he signed that confession. Now I think I know."

"I'm afraid I don't follow you."

"You will. But first I've got a job for you. I never did pay much attention to Moran's will. All I ever knew about it was that Micky Moran inherited her father's entire estate, no strings attached. But I want a copy of that will."

"I'll play the devil getting one. Martel definitely doesn't like us, and the courthouse is closed."

"You'll have to get a clerk from the probate court to open up for you. There's usually a couple of copies filed with the will. If there aren't, make one. I want it to be verbatim."

"All right, but—" Blackie Jones stopped short. Someone had pounded on the side door.

"Open up in the name of the law!"

Mort nodded toward the other door. "Get going. Bring the copy to Russo's office on the boardwalk."

When Blackie Jones had vanished into an outer office Mort crossed to the side door and opened it. Harry Malone and Henney Fielding, the sheriff, strode inside.

"You had your nerve," said Malone, severely, "leaving the scene of the crime. You knew you were a material witness!"

Mort smiled pleasantly. "I was merely trying to help you to apprehend the murderer. It seems you need a little help here lately."

Malone reddened, and Henney Fielding winked behind his back. The sheriff was a big, goodhumored man, quite content with his job and lacking in sympathy for the political ambition that made Malone ever anxious to crowd him out of the spotlight. Mort indicated chairs for his visitors and offered drinks, which both men refused. Mort put away the bottles without further indulging himself.

"Well, Malone, what do you think I can't tell you that Blackie hasn't already told you? We entered Courtney's cottage together. I couldn't possibly have seen anything that he didn't."

"I'm not so sure about that," said Henney Fielding. "You might have seen several things that that kid would pass up."

"Well, I didn't. You can save your time and mine by accepting that as a fact."

"You ran right over to Miss Moran's house," Malone accused.

"Sure, but that wasn't because of the body we found. I was trying to find out something about that fifty-thousand-dollar withdrawal you kept out of the evidence in Courtney's trial."

Again Malone reddened, but he came back angrily: "I had a right to keep that out. Some dumb juror might have got it in his head that a thug knocked off Moran for the money. Besides, it had no material connection with the case."

"I disagree."

Henney Fielding had been studying Mort. "If you've got an idea, I wish you'd spill it."

"I will, in due course."

Malone scowled. "You've no right to withhold evidence!"

"No, but my theories are my own private property. When I've got the evidence to back them up, you can have it. In the meantime, bring me a copy of Blackie's statement with respect to the discovery of the body, and I'll sign it. You can leave the front way if you like, but I suggest the side door because it's quicker."

Malone seemed to be on the verge of a stroke. Without a word he rose and strode to the side door. Henney Fielding threw a wink over his shoulder as he followed. Mort grinned as the door closed behind the pair. He got out the bottle of bourbon and poured a liberal drink. He then phoned Milligan's saloon and ordered a steak.

IT WAS ten o'clock when Mort had finished the steak and the liquid refreshments that made it appetizing. He then leisurely summoned a cab and by a display of generosity persuaded the driver to haul him to Prescott Lake.

The big boardwalk was in full swing when Mort left the cab at its entrance. A rollercoaster car roared around a bend approximating the racket of a subway express train passing through a local station. The shrill percussion music of a merry-go-round, Ferris wheel and other rides made up an ever rising crescendo. Barkers held forth in front of the various concessions, extolling the games playable for one dime, ten cents. Mort proceeded through the crowd, stopped short abreast of the raffle-wheel booth operated so effectively by the luscious blond Winnie.

Blackie Jones was drooling over the counter, and Winnie was neglecting her customers. Mort crossed toward the duo, and Winnie, seeing him, nudged Blackie. The youth straightened, turned about and turned slightly pink.

"That's right, Blackie," said Mort soothingly. "Always combine business with pleasure. Did you get that thing?"

Blackie nodded, reached into his inside coat pocket but Mort stopped him.

"Hold it, Blackie. We've another job to do. Come along."

With an apologetic look to Winnie, Blackie followed him away. Mort's destination was the boardwalk office. Russo was busy inside with two girls making book entries. He smiled a welcome.

"Are you real busy?" Mort asked. "I'd like to borrow your office."

"Anything you ask. Come on, girls, we'll take a walk."

"No, I don't want you to leave, Russo. I want you to do me another favor. Can you have Hal Caldwell come here?"

"Sure thing. The band will sound better without him." He nodded to one of the girl. "You'll want to dance anyway. Tell Caldwell to come on the run."

The girls left. Russo eyed Mort interestedly.

"Now what? Or is your business with Caldwell a military secret?"

"Not from you, Russo. What I'm going to pull may not be exactly regular. Any time you object, say so."

"Shoot the works. I'll back you up to the limit."

Caldwell evidently had much respect for an order from Russo. He appeared in a matter of seconds, stopped short as he beheld Mort. He frowned.

"Say, what is this, Russo? What's this guy doing here? He's Courtney's lawyer."

Russo shrugged and indicated the floor was Mort's. Mort smiled.

"I merely wanted to ask you a question or two, Caldwell."

Caldwell retreated a step toward the door, but no farther. Blackie had effectively blocked it. Fear spread on Caldwell's face.

"What are you trying to do to me? You can't get away with this?"

"Now that's the wrong attitude, Caldwell, I'm only trying to get some information that will help to solve the murders of Jim Moran and Perry Courtney."

Caldwell looked at him as if he thought he were crazy. "That's simple enough! Courtney murdered Moran, then killed himself. Everybody knows that!"

"Sure, and at one time everybody knew the world was flat. I think I can prove who really did murder both men if you'll be helpful. For example, I want you to tell me how long you'd been blackmailing Moran."

Caldwell started, then paled. "That's a damned lie!"

"Come now, Caldwell. Nobody as ignorant of music as you could have fronted a band for Moran unless you'd had something really bad on him. Was it murder?"

Perspiration formed on Caldwell's temples. "You're crazy! You can't prove anything on me! What are you trying to do, make me the goat for the Moran killing?"

"No. I promise you that if you'll give me the facts, I'll never repeat them. That goes for Blackie here, and Russo. Right, Russo?"

Russo nodded. "You know me, Hal. If you've got something, let Mort have it. He's a square-shooter—*I know.*"

Caldwell remained unconvinced. His face was now wet with sweat.

"You let me out of here!" he told Blackie. "If you don't I'll have you arrested. Why, this is kidnaping!"

"Not quite, Caldwell," said Mort soothingly. "Suppose we try an easier question. We happen to know the answer to this one. You did know Happy Kappel wore a tattoo identical to Moran's, didn't you?"

All the blood left Caldwell's face. His voice became shrill. "How did you know that?" He caught himself. "No, I never knew anything of the kind! You can't prove I did!"

Mort shook his head sadly. "I see you're going to be difficult. Blackie, do you remember what you did to that big bruiser who was going to beat up on me in a saloon a couple of weeks ago? Show Caldwell, will you?"

IN WHAT seemed to be one fluid movement Caldwell was lifted from his feet and stretched across Blackie's abdomen. Blackie's arms bent the band leader backwards. The band leader screamed.

"Not quite so hard for the time being anyway," said Mort. Blackie loosened his grip slightly, and Caldwell's screams subsided into whining sobs. "Now, Caldwell, you must know that Blackie could break your back by the application of a little more pressure. I hope that doesn't happen. But if it does, nobody will ever know it happened, for we'll profit from the lesson learned from Moran's murder and see that you never, never come to the surface of Prescott

Lake. As for your screaming, don't think you can ever make yourself heard above that din outside. You haven't a chance, Caldwell. Why don't you answer my questions?"

Blackie punctuated Mort's sentence by the discreet application of pressure.

Caldwell screamed: "All right, let me down, for God's sake! I'll tell you anything you want to know!"

Blackie deposited his burden right-side-up. Caldwell, shaken, rubbed his back, bending over and groaning. Unashamedly he wiped tears from his eyes. He glared at Russo.

"Damn you, Russo! You're to blame for this!"

Russo said: "Tell the man what you know."

"Begin with the tattoo on Happy's chest," said Mort. "It was identical to Moran's, wasn't it?"

Caldwell seemed to be a little puzzled. "Sure, but—"

"That's enough on that. Now tell us what you had on Moran. It was murder, wasn't it?"

"Sure. It happened a hell of a long time ago, but he was still wanted. My old man gave me the lowdown. He was working with a carnival with Moran. They were both just kids then. Moran was a shark at the shell game, and one night a mark he'd taken laid for him. The mark had a knife. Moran had a knife, too. He carved the mark. Too much. The mark croaked.

"It turned out the mark was a local bigshot. Moran killed him in self-defense, but he wouldn't have stood a chance in the county court. He had to lam, and he's been on the lam ever since. They'd still have given him at least life back there if they'd ever caught up with him. The mark's family is still plenty influential."

"And how long had you been blackmailing Moran?"

Caldwell looked around with hesitation until his gaze fell on Blackie. Resignedly, he said: "I wouldn't hardly call it blackmail. I only asked him to give me a job—"

"A job you've no business having," Mort cut in, "I'd figured that's why you rated being a band leader. Now, let's save time. Besides the job, you kept chiseling Moran right along. Then finally you told him that for fifty thousand you'd let him alone for good, right?"

Caldwell looked as if he had been struck. He emphatically shook his head.

"I never did!"

Blackie swung him from the floor again. Caldwell shrieked: "Yes, I did try to take him for fifty grand, but I never got it! I never killed him, either! Somebody killed him before I could collect! Put me down! Mr. Mort, make him put me down!"

Mort nodded, and the band leader was again righted.

Russo had been silent until now. He said: "I never would have believed it! I thought maybe the little punk was a relative or something. Five will get you ten he croaked Moran himself. Maybe even Courtney!"

THE DOOR suddenly opened behind Blackie. Winnie stepped inside. Blackie moved gallantly to permit her entrance. Caldwell saw his chance. He darted for the door so fast that even Blackie couldn't grab him.

Russo snapped: "That was a bright one, Winnie! What do you want?"

Winnie scowled. "Kiazeep yiazour shiazirt iazon! Thiazere's iaza miazark wiazith iaza biazeef!"

"O.K.," Russo said sourly. He addressed Mort. "Got a little business out at Winnie's booth. Won't be a minute. Make yourselves at home."

He left with Winnie.

Mort said: "That's the second time today I've heard that carnie lingo. I wonder how they do it."

"That's easy," said Blackie self-consciously. "While I was waiting for you Winnie told me all about it. They just insert three letters, i-a-z, before every vowel sound. It garbles up even the simplest word so the marks—that's the suckers—can't tell what they're talking about."

"So? What did Winnie tell Russo?"

"She told him to keep his shirt on, that a mark had a beef. In carnival lingo a mark with a beef is a sucker who's decided not to be a sucker and wants his money back. Russo will go out there and settle the beef by paying at least part of the man's losses."

"Well, you learn something every day. Now that we've got a moment to ourselves, suppose you read me Moran's will. Skip the sound-mind-and-body clause and the payment-of-all-just-debts clause."

Blackie got out a copy of folded legal-cap. "I had to slip the clerk a ten-spot for getting this. And he said it would mean his job if it ever got out."

"It won't, and you'll get your ten. Go ahead and read."

"Well, let's see, here's Item Three. It reads:

"All the property, real and personal, of every kind and description, wheresoever situated, which I may own or have the right to dispose of at the time of my decease, I give, bequeath and devise to Louise (Micky) Moran, who has stayed loyally by me in my home, and who has been a source of constant solace to me at all times, absolutely and in fee simple.

"Item Four. I hereby—"

"That's enough!" Mort snapped. "My hunch was right. I only hope it isn't too late!"

"Too late? I don't—"

"Come on, Blackie! We've no time to lose!" He started for the door. It opened and Russo entered, scowling.

"That Winnie! I think she must have been listening outside and pulled a gag to let Caldwell loose. There's wasn't any beef at her pitch when I got there, and I don't think there ever was one!"

Mort said: "You've got a gun?"

"Sure."

"Get it and come with us."

CHAPTER SIX
DIAZOUBLECRIAZOSSING RIAZAT

WHEN THE trio reached Blackie's car, the big fellow said: "Maybe I'll get there quicker if you tell me where we're going."

"The Moran house, of course. Don't you realize her life's in increasing danger every second?"

Blackie's big jaw hung open, but he sent the car away fast.

Russo said: "I don't make it. Mort. Something come up while I was gone?"

"The payoff piece of this jig-saw puzzle. What an idiot I was not to figure it out before!"

Blackie growled: "I wonder what that makes me. I've been right with you all the time, and I still don't know what the hell's going on!"

"You will. Just keep this buggy on its wheels till we get to Micky Moran's!"

The car was on two wheels as it slid into the Moran drive. The house was lighted. Mort raced up the steps, pounded with irritation when he found the screen door locked. An elderly lady approached. She eyed Mort with annoyance.

"Yes?"

"Miss Moran. I must see her."

"Well, she isn't here. She just left."

"Where?"

"That I can't tell you."

"But you've *got* to. It's a matter of life and death—her life!"

The woman looked him over speculatively, then frowned in worry. "Why, what's wrong? She—"

"Haven't you any idea? Don't you know where she'd be likely to go?"

"Why, no. Unless it would be over to the boardwalk."

"We've just left there. We'd have seen her. Think, woman! Isn't there anything that would give you an indication as to where she went?"

"Well, no. I do remember she asked me to hunt up a flashlight, but that's all."

Mort thought this over. Then he slapped a fist in the palm of a hand. He whirled. Blackie and Russo stood behind him. They eyed him blankly.

"Yes, that has to be it! She's driven over to Courtney's cottage! She's looking for that fifty thousand, I'll bet a million! Come on, Blackie, and don't spare the horses!"

Blackie didn't spare the cylinders. In a matter of a very few minutes he again did his two-wheel act, skidding this time into the drive of Courtney's cottage. It was dark.

"Malone or the sheriff will have the keys," Mort said. "My guess is she went in through a window."

"You seem to be pretty sure she's there," Russo said. He sounded skeptical.

"She has to be! You fellows go around the other side, and I'll see what I can do with this side door. Look for jimmied windows!"

Blackie and Russo obeyed. Mort advanced to the side door. In spite of the darkness, he saw that it was open. The lock had been crudely burst. Mort advanced warily in the darkness. He halted when he heard voices, then advanced even more cautiously, moving the length of the living room.

He couldn't see the man who was talking. The man held a flashlight focused on Micky Moran. Her face was the color of death in its yellow glow. She didn't see Mort. She seemed hypnotized by the man with the light, able only to listen.

"You're not very bright," he was saying, "to think Courtney had the fifty grand. You were even dumber to think he killed Jim Moran. It was just a trick to get rid of Caldwell. When Courtney went to Moran's office that night, Moran told him how Caldwell was blackmailing him. Courtney said he'd be crazy to pay the fifty thousand, for Caldwell would always come back for more money.

"He said it would be best for Moran to take the money and run away and start all over. Jim objected to that, arguing that Caldwell would follow him. Courtney told him there was one way out. He could convince Caldwell that he was dead. Jim asked him how that could be done, and Courtney told him. He—"

"I'll take it on from there," said Mort, stepping into the room. For an instant the flashlight played upon him, then the voice said: "Stand by the girl, wise guy!"

Mort complied. "Anything to oblige, Happy. I've never seen you nor have I ever heard your voice, but you have to be Happy Kappel. Do you mind if I tell the rest of your story?"

"Go ahead, wise guy. It'll be the last time you'll ever tell it!"

"I'll leave that to fate." Mort turned to the startled Micky Moran. "You see, Courtney happened to be very much in love with you. Enough to sign a confession to a murder he didn't commit. It was the one way to convince Caldwell that Jim Moran was dead. Moran agreed only upon the condition that he stick around in hiding so that he could put in an appearance if a jury did happen to convict Courtney.

"After Courtney was in the clear, Moran was to take his fifty thousand, go away somewhere and start all over under an assumed name. You'd be left in good shape with a valuable resort property. It really wasn't a bad way out for Moran, though Courtney had to take an awful beating, having you think he murdered your father.

"He was willing to do it, though, because he was in love. Everything would have gone as planned if Jim Moran hadn't talked to his oldest friend and told him the whole story. I mean Happy Kappel, of course. I knew they were bosom friends when I found out that they had identical tattoo marks. When two people wear the same tattoo, it means they had the job done together, and that means they're pals from way back.

"They'd gone different ways, Happy and Jim. Happy was just an old carnie while Jim was a big operator. He gave Happy a petty job, and Happy seemed grateful enough. But Jim didn't quite appreciate Happy. Happy had ambitions of his own. I don't just mean the fifty thousand dollars. Of course Happy took that after he killed Jim. But he had a better motive for murder than that.

"He wanted to own the whole boardwalk with the hotel, night club and Jim's interest in the Palace. To do it he had only to kill two people, Jim and you, Micky!"

The girl's eyes were incredulous.

"But that's not true! How could Happy get the boardwalk by killing me? Why, we're not even related!"

"I'm afraid you are, Micky. Legally, at any rate. I realized that when I found out exactly how Jim Moran's will was worded. He was careful not to refer to you as his daughter. He was equally careful to identify you as the Micky Moran who had stayed in his home, so that you could legally inherit his estate. No, Micky, you weren't even Jim Moran's adopted daughter!"

"But—but then who am I supposed to be?"

Mort said: "I'll let you tell her, Happy."

The man invisible behind the flashlight said: "Legally you're my child, but I always knew better. I guessed that much from the beginning, and when Jim suggested he let me raise you, I knew. What's more. I can prove you're my legal child by your birth certificate. When your body turns up in the lake, I'll step in and claim all your estate."

Micky Moran said: "That's not true! It isn't really, is it, Mr. Mort?"

"I'm afraid it is. I knew Happy had to act quickly because you might write a will if he waited too long. At your death he'll inherit everything you got from Jim Moran. You can see that the stakes were high in this game."

"And I've played it smart," boasted Happy Kappel. "I killed Jim the night Courtney confessed he did, and kept him in the lake where he couldn't be found. Then, after Courtney was acquitted today I towed him out where a fisherman could find him at the place Courtney said he dropped him."

"That was indeed clever," Mort conceded. "You knew that if the body was found before Courtney was acquitted, he'd blurt out the truth. So you waited until the trial was over, knowing Courtney couldn't believe Moran's body was actually found. I was right when I guessed that Courtney left Milligan's Saloon to find out if the body was Moran's. But I was wrong in thinking he'd go to see the body itself. He went to the place where Moran was supposed to be hiding, sure he'd find Moran there. But he didn't. He found you, didn't he, Happy?"

"I'll say he did! Moran was supposed to be hiding here in his own cottage. When Courtney walked in I just knocked him out with a rabbit punch that doesn't show hardly at all and then undressed him and put him in the bathtub. I waited till he was about conscious, then put the gun in his hand. Just as he came to I squeezed his finger on the trigger. That was pretty smart if I do say it. It made it look like suicide all right!"

"Yes, that was pretty smart. But even a dummy like Harry Malone will get wise when Micky comes up in the lake with a bullet in her body. I trust that you do have a gun in your other hand."

"Sure, but you get the bullet, not Micky. I can handle her without a gun. I'll just hold her under water a while, and nature will do the rest. Folks'll say she drowned herself on account of Jim's murder."

"But you'll need a good criminal lawyer, Happy. Can't we make a deal?"

"Shut up! Do you want it in the back, or do you want to take it the way you are now?"

"I don't think I'll take it at all. Look at the window, Happy."

AT FIRST Happy Kappel suspected a trick. Then his eyes caught sight of the face in the window. He whirled and fired. Another gun spoke from the doorway. The flashlight dropped to the floor and rolled.

Mort sprang forward and picked it up. He ran to the window. "You all right Blackie?"

The face reappeared and smiled through the shattered remnants of the glass.

"Sure, only I'm afraid to look at my hat!"

"Come on around. We've got something in here."

Mort turned back and held the flash on the fallen figure. Russo, gun in hand, stared.

"I think I got him dead center. And not a moment too soon!"

"Right. That was good shooting, Russo."

The figure on the floor groaned. Glazing eyes stared upward. They regarded Mort, then Russo. Dying lips trembled, then said: "lazi shiazouldn't hiazave triazusted yiazou, yiazou diazoublecriazossing riazat!"

Mort rose when he heard a scuffling sound.

"Blackie, what the devil are you doing?"

"Nailing the big brain behind Happy's scheme," Blackie said. He had disarmed Russo and held him perfectly powerless. "I never thought that old goat had the brains to figure out such a murder scheme. Russo did it for him, then shot him to shut him up when the game was up. I suppose the deal was for them to split the loot."

"But, Blackie, how can you know that! You can't prove it!"

"Sure," snarled Russo, "he's off his nut!"

Blackie said, tightening his grip on Russo: "We've got a dying declaration, C.D. You heard what Happy said. It explains why Russo killed him."

"Dying declaration? That was gibberish!"

"No, it wasn't. It was carnie, the lingo that Happy and Russo both knew. Even though Russo shot him, Happy wasn't going to squeal. He had to get Russo told off, so he told him in carnie, thinking we wouldn't understand it."

"All right, translate what he said."

"He said: "I shouldn't have trusted you, you double-crossing rat!""

Russo snarled: "You can't make anything out of that! You can't prove I had anything to do with either Moran's or Courtney's murder! Why, I saved this guy's life, killing Happy!"

Mort said: "Don't let him go yet. Make him tell you where his share of those fifty thousand-dollar bills is. The bank has their numbers, and that'll cinch the case."

It took Blackie only forty seconds to get the truth out of Russo, who had already seen what happened to Caldwell. Micky did not look away. She seemed to enjoy it.

"I can't apologize too much," she told Mort later during a light supper in her bungalow, "for the way I treated you."

"Don't thank me, thank Blackie for being able to understand carnie and translate Happy's last words. He must have picked it up awfully quick."

"It isn't everybody who can have a teacher like Winnie. You should look her up and thank her, Blackie."

Blackie scowled. "I forgot to mention it. She told me she was going to marry that blackmailing band leader. They're probably over the state line by now."

Mort sighed. "It's all for the best, Blackie. Stay a bachelor, and you'll never be lonely."

MOSTLY FOR MURDER

CLARENCE DARROW MORT COULDN'T UNDERSTAND HIS PARTNER'S SUDDEN INTEREST IN PISTOL SHOOTING, UNLESS HE FELT HE NEEDED PROTECTION FROM THE CHARACTERS WHO WALKED INTO MORT'S OFFICE AS FELONS AND WALKED OUT AS CLIENTS. BUT PERHAPS BLACKIE JONES WAS RIGHT IN BEING CAUTIOUS. TYLER FENWICK HADN'T BEEN—THOUGH NOW HE WAS TOO DEAD TO CARE.

CLARENCE DARROW MORT, known familiarly, if not affectionately, as "Corpus Delicti" Mort, picked up a paperweight from his desk and threw it at the frosted glass of his door. His aim was perfect. The glass exploded from its frame and fell in a thousand fragments to the floor of the reception room outside. After a discrete interval the face of Miss Blimm, Mort's secretary, appeared in the frame.

"What is it this time, Mr. Mort?"

"Never you mind. Find me Blackie Jones."

"Yes, Mr. Mort."

Mort listened to the repeated dialing of Miss Blimm's phone. Presently she became engaged in a conversation with someone who apparently was deaf.

"It's Blackie Jones I want!" Miss Blimm screamed. "Blackstone Jones, if you want his whole name. He's a lawyer, the junior partner of Mort & Jones!"

The scream failed to register, and Miss Blimm repeated, still louder. There was a pause. Then Miss Blimm yelled: "Get right over here, Mr. Jones! It's something serious!"

Miss Blimm hung up. Mort eyed her through his shattered door frame.

"Is everybody stricken deaf, or did you just get a bad connection?"

"Neither. I found Mr. Jones at his usual hangout, a shooting gallery."

Mort's brow lifted.

"Usual? How long has this been going on?"

"About two weeks."

"Some blonde running the shooting gallery?"

"No. Mr. Jones has taken up pistol shooting. I think that's what's made him so irritable lately. It seems that after two weeks he can't hit anything but the backstop."

"Now why would Blackie go in for pistol shooting?"

"I don't know unless it's because he feels he needs some protection from the characters who walk in here as felons and walk out as clients."

Mort frowned. "I think, Miss Blimm, I have observed before that my clientele cannot be expected to be enlisted from the ranks of the Union League Club. I wouldn't want them to be. In fact, something has just happened to make me feel that my criminal clients differ from their more respectable contemporaries only in that, when all is said and done, they do possess a certain innate decency."

Miss Blimm maintained a superior silence. She busied herself with picking up the pieces of glass from Mort's door. Mort returned to his desk, at which he sat dejectedly, his eyes fixed upon the folded sheaf of paper lying there.

He was still staring at the paper five minutes later when Blackie Jones walked into the room. Blackie had to stoop. His six feet-seven inches of height, which had kept him out of the Army, also kept him on constant guard against doorways constructed for comparative midgets like Mort, who was over a foot shorter.

"Well, C.D., what's all the rush about? Somebody get himself bumped off?"

"No, but somebody should. I refer specifically to Cornelius C. Newhall, of the law firm of Newhall, Newhall & Carter. Look at this."

Blackie picked up the paper which had caused Mort's outburst and ran his eyes over it rapidly. He turned his gaze incredulously upon Mort.

"Why, the dirty rat! I wouldn't have thought that possible of him!"

Mort shrugged. "I'll confess I was fooled. Every so often I slip up and overestimate human character. I should have known that Corny Newhall would stoop to anything to pick up a fee, but I thought he had enough professional feeling not to try to pull anything like this. Yet, here he is, two days before Bevans was to get his deed, suing for cancellation!"

"Why, he's practically accusing you of aiding and abetting Jack Bevans in getting that Brownell woman drunk and making her sign a contract!"

"Of course. I told him he'd have to make a liar out of me if he hoped to prove the Brownell woman had even had a drink when she signed that contract. Corny said he wouldn't try anything like that. But evidently he's changed his mind. Mrs. Brownell probably upped the ante."

Blackie's brows arched. He shook his head.

"No, I don't think she's the one paying the fee. I think it's the rest of the people in Fairfax Heights. They're so set on keeping Bevans out of there they'd probably take up a collection to hire lawyers to prevent him from living there."

"Well, they're not going to get away with it! Mrs. Brownell sold her house to Bevans for seventy-five thousand when fifty was all anybody else would pay. He had to,

Out of the darkness came a flash of light, simultaneous with a sharp report. Bevans pitched forward. A bullet cracked the air.

to overcome her personal pride. She knew what all of her society friends would say if she let a slot machine racketeer into exclusive Fairfax Heights. But she didn't think so much of what they would say that she could turn down an offer like the one Bevans made. The contract price in itself shows that Mrs. Brownell was cold sober at the time."

Blackie frowned. "It does to you, and it does to me, but other people may look at it differently. They may feel that Mrs. Brownell wouldn't have sold to Bevans under any circumstances unless she was too drunk to know what she was doing. And the undisputed fact is that she is a lush. If she's not stewed to the gills, it's an exceptional occasion."

"This was such an occasion. I wish you had been in the office at the time. But Miss Blimm was, also Miss Patterson. They'll testify that Mrs. Brownell was completely sober."

"Sure, but they work for you. Their testimony will be discounted because of that."

"True, but there'll be my testimony. As I told Corny Newhall, he'll have to make a liar out of me."

BLACKIE SIGHED. "Well, I really didn't expect that of him. Why, his firm's the most reputable civil practice firm in town! Corny's a member of all the swank clubs, chairman of a dozen committees and president of the Bar Association!"

"He's still a frustrated porch-climber. There are times when I feel like retiring from the legal profession and leaving it to the hyenas that now infest it. For years I've maintained the preposterous fiction that members of the bar are a nobler breed than other men, that they are unjustly painted as shysters and poltroons. Alas, I must say, after all these years, that it's easier for a sinner to get in heaven than an honest man into the profession!"

Blackie looked shocked. "You can't mean that, C.D.!"

"The hell I can't! More lawyers would tell the truth if it weren't for the fact that they can be disbarred for doing so. As you know, one ground for disbarment is maligning the profession. Hypocrisy is therefore enforced by the strictest of penalties. Let an honest man wander by mistake into the ranks of the profession and voice his revulsion at what he finds, and he is booted out in disgrace by the entire gang of sublimated purse-snatchers."

"I can't think you really believe that, C.D. You're just in a temper about what old Corny Newhall has done. You should remember that he's not representative of the profession. Everybody in the bar knows that he's an over-rated stuffed shirt and that he's so greedy he suffers tortures when any other firm makes a dollar. These Fairfax Heights people have dangled enough money in front of his nose to make him try to upset that contract even at the cost of disgracing you."

"Well, he won't upset it. I don't blame the Heights people for not wanting Jack Bevans in their midst, but I do blame them for their tactics in trying to keep him out. I'll give them a run for their money!" Mort pressed a button on his inter-office communication phone and snapped: "Miss Blimm, get me Jack Bevans."

Seconds elapsed, then a buzzer sounded, and Mort picked up his phone.

"Hello, Jack. Has a deputy been around yet with a summons? No? Well, one will be. Mrs. Brownell's sued for cancellation of her contract on the ground that she was stung at the time. No, of course she won't get away with it. The Heights people are the ones fighting it, though, and they'll put up plenty of dough to hire witnesses to testify that Mrs. Brownell hadn't drawn a sober breath for weeks. It'll be a swearing match! I'm putting Blackie to work on the evidence now. No, I don't need you, but I do need the five hundred you'll have to put up. Thanks, I'll have Miss Blimm give your messenger a receipt."

Mort hung up and turned to Blackie.

"Don't spare the horses. This is one case I want to win if it costs me ten times my fee. Civil cases are a little out of my line, but evidence is evidence, and I'm counting on you to get it for me. The best place to begin with is how

Mrs. Brownell spent the day on which she signed that contract. The file will show you when it was. I want everything complete. Hire the Mayhew Agency and tell them to put as many men as necessary on it. And keep them on it!"

Blackie nodded. Mort rose from his chair, walked out into the reception room, which was by now almost free of broken glass, and got his hat. He failed to speak to Olie, his favorite elevator man, and similarly insulted half a dozen other passengers on the elevator, two of whom were clients.

Downstairs he got his car from its lot and drove aimlessly. It always helped to settle his nerves, just driving. Something in the eight-cylindered purr of the motor acted as an analgesic to his soul. Perhaps, he thought, it was because a machine was relatively dependable, a thing that under the same circumstances could be counted upon to perform the same way.

As usual, he drove to Scioto Road, a beautiful super-highway stretching along a river of the same name that shone brightly under the slanting rays of the afternoon sun. Mort drove ten miles, then turned in to a wayside bar and diluted his anger with beer.

He had finished his second bottle and was getting up from his booth when she came in. He hoped she wouldn't see him, but she did and came right over.

"Hello, Mr. Mort. I spotted your car and stopped just to talk to you."

"Sorry, Miss Brownell, I was just leaving."

"But this is important. I know what Mother's done. I think it's terrible. I want to do everything I can to help you."

Mort sat back in his booth. The girl took a place opposite him. If you looked closely enough you could see a resemblance between Shirley Brownell and her mother. She would probably look exactly like the older woman if she drank liquor fast enough until she reached her mother's age. At the present moment, however, she was as beautiful a brown-haired creature as Mort had ever laid eyes on.

"I don't understand, Miss Brownell. Why do you want to help me win against your mother?"

"Because it's simply disgraceful, what she's trying to do! Imagine, going into court with witnesses to testify that she's a chronic alcoholic and was practically dead drunk when she sold the house my father left her!"

"I see your point. I hadn't given the matter enough thought to reflect on how it would look from your viewpoint. From mine, it doesn't look so good. It's not very pleasant to have somebody charge that I permit irresponsible drunken people to transact business in my law office."

"Of course not! I'm sure even Mother appreciates that. But those Heights people forced her into it. They made her feel she'd committed some horrible crime selling a plot of ground in the sacred precincts of Fairfax Heights!"

Mort reflected and said: "It would help if we could prove that. I would show that your mother isn't the real party-in-interest to the suit."

"If you think so, I'll do anything to help. I already know, for instance, that Tyler Fenwick is the ringleader of the Heights group. You know him, of course."

"I've had the honor. I helped carry him to a cab the night he was blackjacked at the Lucky Club. He'd lost more than usual, and when he took a swing at the croupier, he got in the way of the billy."

"Sounds like him. He hates anyone who knows how to make money instead of just inheriting it the way he did. And his pal, Jock Martel, is in the scheme almost as deep as he is in debt. All he has left is a place in the Heights, and there's a mortgage on that."

"I know Jock, too. He ranks high in any 'Booze Who.' So they're the guys who think Jack Bevans would be a menace to their neighborhood!"

"Oh, there are others, of course. Take Jimmy Carnes, the boy I'm going to marry if he ever gets back from the South Pacific. His mother told me the family would definitely move out of the Heights if Bevans moved in."

"Well, I can understand the attitude of people like that. But they're going to take Bevans and like it. Now, about this group of people fighting him, is it organized?"

"No. They just get together at Tyler Fenwick's place. They had a meeting last night. Afterwards Tyler and a few of his friends knocked themselves out with some black-market liquor Jock had dug up somewhere. It was real Scotch, but it cost Jock a hundred and fifty a case."

"You were there?"

"Of course not! I wouldn't be caught dead at one of Tyler's brawls. The only woman who stayed after the meeting was Sylvia Farrell. She's been trying to marry Tyler, and she'll keep on trying even if he sprouts a second head."

"Well, it would be interesting to have a transcript of what happened at that meeting. But I imagine any dirty work, such as hiring witnesses, will be left to an inner circle."

"I think that might be what the gang stayed to work out last night. Imagine it, plotting to prove that my mother was drunk, always has been a drunkard and always will be!"

She stopped abruptly, and Mort looked away, for a woman in tears pained him.

Finally she composed herself, and Mort said: "I'll leave this thing up to the detective agency that does my work. Maybe they can plant a dictograph in Fenwick's home."

"I'll even help do that if I can."

MORT WAITED until she had driven away, then went to his car and drove back to his office. For the first time in his career he was in a client's shoes. Always before he had stood by with the calm detachment of an attorney, amused by his client's ill-concealed concern. Now, because his own reputation was at stake, he was more uneasy than the most troubled of his clients.

Blackie Jones was on the telephone when Mort walked into Blackie's private office. It was after closing hours, but Miss Blimm was still on the job outside. Mort grunted: "Well?"

Blackie Jones looked worried.

"I've checked with the Recorder's office. I don't suppose you remember, but just before Bevans was supposed to come over here with Mrs. Brownell, he went with her to the Recorder's office, where they recorded a certified copy of Mrs. Brownell's divorce decree. I had advised Bevans to have that done. Remember?"

"I remember Bevans saying they'd just been to the Recorder's office."

"Well, Miss Blimm's record shows they arrived here at ten-fifty-one in the morning. The carbon copy of the receipt the Recorder's clerk gave Mrs. Brownell shows they were there at nine-thirty-five."

Mort looked stunned. "Then they were an hour and sixteen minutes getting here from the courthouse, six blocks away!"

"So it seems. Of course the clerk could have made a mistake, but that seems hardly likely. There's an inference that the pair stopped on the way, and they could have stopped at a saloon. You can get awfully drunk in an hour, allowing sixteen minutes to get here."

Mort strode to the reception room door.

"Get me Bevans."

Miss Blimm reached for her phone, then stopped. Jack Bevans had come into the room. He saw Mort and strode sullenly toward him.

Mort said: "Why didn't you tell me it took you and Mrs. Brownell an hour to get here from the courthouse the day she signed that contract?"

"You're crazy! It didn't? Who says so?"

"The Recorder's clerk."

"Then he's a liar. We walked right here. I want to see you in your private office."

Mort ushered his client to his private office. Inside, Bevans seemed about to go to pieces. Mort regarded him closely.

"This seems to have upset you considerably. Where's the famous Jack Bevans grin?"

Bevans remained grim.

"It's not the Brownell deal, C.D. It's something worse. It's murder."

"Whose?"

"Tyler Fenwick's."

"The hell you say! Read it in the papers?"

"No. I just left his place in the Heights. I've known all along that he was the ringleader of the mob trying to keep me out of there. After you called me this afternoon I sat there stewing about it and finally I got mad. So I drove out to Fenwick's for a showdown."

"What did you kill him with?"

"Can the kidding. I didn't kill him. Someone else had got to him first—with a bottle of Scotch. A full bottle. The blow didn't break it, but it crushed the back of Fenwick's head. The bottle was lying there beside him—it had to be the murder weapon."

"How'd you happen to find him?"

"Well, I figured the servants wouldn't let me in if I went to the front door, so I pulled up in the drive and went around to a terrace. A French door was open, and I walked right in. It was a dumb thing to do, but I was mad. The first thing I came across was Fenwick lying there with his head conked in. I gave him a look-over to see if he was still alive, then I beat it right out when I saw he wasn't."

"Leave any prints?"

"You know me better than that. But I'm marked. A gardener saw me leave. It'll just be a matter of time. That's why I need you."

Mort sighed. "I'm afraid you do. You had a motive, and you've got a temper. Your reputation as a racketeer will do the rest."

"That's not fair. I never was a racketeer. I always bought my protection. I never used a muscle man in my life."

"But the public has other ideas, and a jury is drawn from the public."

Bevans made a wry face. "Well, I suppose it's going to cost me."

"It really will, Jack."

"You think I ought to turn myself in? That gardener will put the finger on me quick enough once the body's discovered."

"Maybe. But perhaps all he can do is give a vague description."

"I'm afraid I'm a notorious guy, C.D. Besides, he could have spotted the plates on my car."

"I think that's doubtful. I suggest that we go over there now and see if anybody's stumbled across the body."

Bevans shrugged. "Anything you say."

They left Mort's office. He stuck his head inside Blackie's office. "There's been a new development. You'll find it on the electronic machine."

Bevans gave Mort a double-take. "You got all that on wax?"

"Sure. Any objections?"

"I guess not. If I can't trust you, I might as well throw in the sponge."

TWENTY MINUTES later, Mort turned into Fairfax Heights, and two minutes after that they pulled into the Fenwick drive. He nodded to Bevans. The two men crossed to the front door. Mort rang. A maid answered.

"Mr. Fenwick, please. Mr. Mort and Mr. Bevans calling."

The maid started to close the door.

"Just a minute, please. Here comes another visitor, I think."

A second car had entered the drive. It stopped. Jock Martel got out. Martel staggered slightly as he started toward the door. Mort turned back to the maid.

"You can announce Mr. Martel also."

The maid waited, holding the door.

"Come right on in, Mr. Martel."

Martel passed by Mort and Bevans as if he had never seen them before in his life. He was a too-handsome man, perhaps thirty, though dissipation and the effects of too-soft living made him look older. Mort regarded Bevans and took a deep breath.

"Well, it won't be long now."

"No. In about a second we'll hear the maid yell."

But there was no yell. Seconds passed. The door opened. Jack Martel looked out sullenly.

"Come in, you."

Mort and Bevans entered. They silently followed Martel to a sitting room with French doors opening onto the terrace Bevans had described. Tyler Fenwich lay sprawled on the floor. The maid sat in a chair, her mouth open.

"What did you fellows want with Tyler?" Jock Martel asked.

"I don't think that's any of your business," Mort told him.

"You'll talk soon enough," Martel snapped. "I've phoned the police."

Mort turned to the maid.

"When did you first discover that Mr. Fenwick was dead?"

"Just now, when I came in here with Mr. Martel."

"Then you hadn't been in this room all afternoon?"

"Not since about four o'clock. Mr. Fenwick said he didn't want to be disturbed."

"Are you the only servant in the house?"

"On Thursdays I am. There's a gardener who works outside."

Martel stepped between the maid and Mort.

"Where do you think you are, Mort, a courtroom?" He spun on the maid. "Don't answer any more of his questions."

"Yes, Mr. Martel."

Mort nodded to Bevans who followed him outside through the big French doorway.

"Where you going?" Martel demanded. Mort didn't answer. He spied the gardener and walked up to him. He introduced himself. The gardener was an elderly man, thin, raw-boned. He pulled off a glove to give Mort a calloused hand. His name was Quigley.

"Mr. Quigley," Mort asked, "did you see anyone enter or leave by the terrace this afternoon?"

"There was this gentleman here. And then there was the lady."

"Who was the lady?"

"I wouldn't know. At first I thought it was Mrs. Brownell. I've often seen her here. But it wasn't her. It was a much younger woman."

"Was she here before or after this gentleman?"

"Before. About ten minutes before, I guess. I wasn't paying much attention, but I saw her leave."

Mort turned to Bevans.

"Come on, Jack. We'll go talk to the lady." Puzzled, Bevans followed him. Martel stood out on the terrace as they came abreast of it.

"You fellows aren't leaving, are you? You better not!"

Without stopping, Mort said: "You can tell the police they can find both Mr. Bevans and myself at my office inside of an hour. We'll be glad to ask any questions then."

In his car, Mort said: "You know where the Brownell place is. Show me the way."

He turned around, squeezed by Martel's car and drove a block as directed. The Brownell place was one of the most elaborate in Fairfax Heights. There was a car in the drive. It was the car Shirley Brownell had driven on Scioto Road earlier in the afternoon.

Mort crossed the lawn, Bevans starting to trail him. Mort turned, held up his hand.

"I'd better handle this, Jack. I know her."

At first a maid told him Miss Brownell couldn't see him. Mort became firm. A few seconds later, Shirley Brownell appeared. Mort followed her into a sitting room.

"Well?"

The girl pretended ignorance. Mort frowned.

"Let's not stall. Quigley, the Fenwick gardener, saw you leave his place this afternoon."

Shirley Brownell had been pale. Now she colored.

"I was afraid he had. I was only in there a moment. I saw Tyler lying there and went right out."

"You had an appointment to see him?"

"No."

"Then why were you there?"

"I got to thinking after my talk with you. On the way back I made up my mind to see Tyler. I thought if I could make him understand how important this whole thing was to me, he'd drop it."

"Just like that!"

This time Shirley Brownell blushed honestly.

"Tyler had a crush on me for a long time. I thought maybe I could influence him."

"But you couldn't because he was beyond influence?"

"Yes. He was really dead, wasn't he?"

"Very. I've been wondering where you got all the lowdown on Fenwick's party last night?"

"Sylvia Farrell told me. I ran into her at a beauty parlor earlier this afternoon."

"Why would she tell you about a brawl like that?"

"To prove to herself that it wasn't anything to be ashamed of. People like Sylvia always talk more than anyone else about their drinking bouts in the attempt to sell themselves the idea that what they're doing is perfectly all right."

"Would Sylvia give you a list of the other male guests at the party?"

"I suppose she would if I got around her in the right way. Do you think one of them might have killed Tyler?"

"I don't think anything, but I want all the information I can get."

"Why are you so concerned? And, come to think of it, how did you know Tyler was dead?"

"I'm representing a client who will, in all probability, be Suspect Number Two."

Shirley Brownell grew thoughtful.

"Who do you think will be Number One?"

"You."

She paled again. Mort went on: "You were there before my client can be placed there, and you had plenty of reason to kill Fenwick. He was using your mother to protect the alleged respectability of his exclusive neighborhood. You knew that he was going to make her go into court and testify that she was a habitual drunkard, too drunk to know what she was doing when she made the deal in my office. You knew Fenwick would drag a roomful of witnesses into court to corroborate her testimony. The thing worked on you. So you went to Fenwick's house. When he refused to drop the idea, you picked up a Scotch bottle and slugged him."

"Do you really think that?"

"It doesn't matter what I think. I'm paid to sponsor any theory of the case that gets an acquittal for my client."

Shirley Brownell jumped up. "I never should have talked to you! I wouldn't have if I hadn't counted on you being my lawyer! You must have known that, and you're taking deliberate advantage of it."

Mort shrugged as he got up. "I stopped trying to read women's minds when I was six years old."

OUTSIDE, HE drove silently from the premises. Bevans said: "Well?"

"I don't know. The gardener saw her leave ten minutes before he saw you leave. But he didn't see either of you arrive—if he had, he would have mentioned it. So the D.A. will argue that you got there ahead of Shirley Brownell, committed the dastardly deed and hid when she arrived."

"So Shirley Brownell was the woman Quigley saw!"

"Didn't you guess? He said he thought it was Mrs. Brownell at first, then he realized it was a much younger woman. It had to be Shirley."

"She didn't say she saw my car in the drive, did she?"

"I didn't ask her. Hasn't it occurred to you the D.A. will argue that you parked somewhere else at first, killed Fenwick, then later pulled into the drive where the gardener would be sure to see you and testify that you left after the girl did?"

"No, I didn't think of that."

"Well, I'm paid to think of things like that."

"You don't really think that's the way it happened, do you?"

"I don't know. Whether or not you killed Tyler Fenwick makes no difference to me as your lawyer. The Constitution of the United States assures every accused man the right of counsel. It doesn't say that he has the right only when he tells his lawyer he's innocent. If you are guilty, say so. You've got two strikes against you if you don't level with your lawyer."

"Well, I've leveled."

"Fine. We'll go back to my office and face the music."

Mort's reception room contained two plain-clothesmen. Mort tried to keep his smile from looking over-done.

"Glad to see you, Captain Merica. And I'm even happier that you're in charge of this case. I know we can count on fair play."

"Cut it out," said Merica. "I didn't wear my rubbers." He was a man of fifty, wearing an American Legion button and a wary look. He regarded Mort reproachfully. "You shouldn't have left the scene of the crime."

"I was only trying to be of service to you, Captain. Now, if you'll give me a moment alone with my junior partner, I'll join you in a moment."

Merica opened his mouth to protest, but Mort stepped into Blackie's office before he could speak. Blackie was looking dejectedly out of a window.

"Well?"

"Snyder at the Mayhew Agency reports that Newhall is going to introduce evidence that Mrs. Brownell spent an hour in the Golden Pheasant Club with Bevans on his way to your office. The help there will say that she was so drunk they stopped serving her drinks."

"Let me see, isn't that the place Tyler Fenwick hangs out in?"

"Sure. By the way, it looks as if our client can forget the Brownell case. From where I stand he's really in a jam. I played back your record."

"Did you take it off the machine?"

"Yes. A fresh one's on."

"Good. I'll make a new one of my conversation with Merica. That's why I wanted him here."

Mort stepped through a doorway and into the library that separated Blackie's office from his own. He entered his own office, opened the outer door and said: "Come in, Captain. I'll even furnish my own rubber hose!"

Merica and the other detective entered the room with Mort and Bevans. They sat around Mort's desk while Mort chose his own chair, where his foot could rest on the electronic recorder button.

Mort played it straight across the board, beginning with Bevans' visit and concluding with his interview of Shirley Brownell. Merica listened expressionlessly.

"So it all hinges around this law suit over a contract for Mrs. Brownell's property, doesn't it?"

Mort shrugged. "Not necessarily. A dozen people would have conked Tyler Fenwick for a dozen different reasons. He was a fourteen-carat rat, and he spent every day proving it."

"Well, that would be a coincidence. This Brownell case was filed today, and today Fenwick gets it. That I don't think is a coincidence."

"Suit yourself, Captain. Only you'll be wise in getting a list of names of the people at Fenwick's party last night. I asked Miss Brownell to get it for me, but I'm afraid she won't accommodate me now."

"Oh, I'll get it all right." He turned to Bevans. "I'm not booking you, Bevans. Only don't take any rides."

"He won't," said Mort soothingly. "You can question him whenever you like."

Merica turned a grim look on Mort. "You, too, C.D. For once I'm regarding you as a suspect. This Brownell case made you plenty sore, and you knew Fenwick was behind it. The Brownell girl told you. You could have conked Fenwick yourself."

Mort held his sides as he laughed, but out of the corner of his eye he saw that his client was looking thoughtful.

"You can't be serious, Captain. Why, I talked to the gardener—he didn't recognize me."

"And I saw where the gardener was most of the afternoon. Fifty people could have come in and out without his seeing them."

"Well, if you're so anxious to pin this on a lawyer, how about accepting a nomination from me? I give you the name of Cornelius C. Newhall."

Merica was aghast. "What, the lawyer? You can't be serious!"

"The hell I'm not! Wasn't he representing Mrs. Brownell, and wasn't the Fairfax Heights crowd back of her? Tyler Fenwick was running the show for those people, and it's a cinch he's the man Corny Newhall looked to for his fees. If you think I'm not above suspicion, why give that old duffer a clean bill of health?"

Merica said nothing. He got up, and the second detective followed him. Mort glared as the door closed behind them.

"CAN YOU tie that? Merica thinks just because that psalm-singing old hypocrite changes his halo every morning he's above suspicion! Boy, I'd give a year's fees if it would turn out that Corny Newhall is the killer after all!"

Bevans looked glum. "Well, I'm not fooled a bit. Ten will get you five that I'll still spend the night in the can. Merica would have taken me in now if you hadn't been with me. He'll wait till you're out of sight then yank me off the streets."

"O.K. Maybe you'll be safer in jail."

"What do you mean by that crack?"

"I mean I think Merica had the right hunch when he said Fenwick's murder is tied up with the Brownell deal. I've a little hunch of my own. I don't think the murderer is quite satisfied yet."

Bevans gulped. "You mean—"

Mort nodded. "Now, get the hell out of here, and hole up with some trusted pals where nobody can bend a whiskey bottle over your head. I want to be alone."

Bevans left. Mort crossed the library and into Blackie's office. Blackie said: "Listen to this."

He turned a switch, and a combination loudspeaker and microphone on his desk came alive. A needle scratched on wax. A telephone conversation followed. It was the Mayhew Detective Agency making a report. After preliminary remarks, the report was monotonously droned:

> Investigator Rankin was assigned at 5:10 P.M. to follow Mrs. Brownell. He contacted her at 5:31 P.M. She was in a booth at the Golden Pheasant Club on South Fifth Street. She was intoxicated. Rankin sipped a soft drink while the subject drank two doubleshots of whiskey. The subject then left her booth, walking unsteadily. She took a cab and went home. Rankin followed and took up a station where he could view the front of her house. Subject arrived home at 6:11 P.M. At 6:36 P.M.

a green convertible entered the drive. A girl got out. Rankin doesn't know family, but he thinks the girl was probably Mrs. Brownell's daughter. No one came or left until 7:41 P.M. when C.D. Mort, attorney, and Jack Bevans arrived. Mort went inside, stayed ten minutes, while Bevans remained in car. Both men drove away at 7:52. Rankin reported by phone at 8:30. No other visitors at Bronwell home at that time. Time used is Eastern Standard war time, or city time. Compute one hour slower for state time.

Blackie switched off the machine.

"That's it. What do you think?"

"I think Mrs. Brownell could have gone out the back of her house, traveled a block to Fenwick's place and killed him."

"Why would she kill him?"

"Fenwick or someone in his crowd was using plenty of pressure to get her to file that law suit. No woman wants to go into court and admit by her own testimony and that of others that she is a habitual drunkard. Especially when she has a marriageable daughter. Someone had to force her hand. You know what usually happens to blackmailers."

"But she must have been dead drunk."

"You can never tell about a drunk. She might come to and then, if she remembers killing Fenwick at all, think it's a bad dream."

"You don't really think that."

"No. I don't think it was a drunken brain that disposed of Fenwick. I think someone was using Fenwick, that he wasn't the brain behind this law suit, only a front. Fenwick got wise to the real stakes and said the deal was off. So Fenwick got killed."

Blackie shrugged. "What could the real stakes be? Bevans wants to buy the property at half again what it's worth, and the people out there don't want him to buy it. That's all there is to it. What else could there be?"

"When I find out I'll tell you who killed Tyler Fenwick."

Blackie shrugged. "I'm doing my best. The Mayhew operators are working on the Golden Pheasant angle. If the help there are on the level about Mrs. Brownell getting drunk in the place, then it looks bad. That hour and sixteen minutes gave the gal plenty of time to get plastered."

"Doesn't Rocky Romano own the Golden Pheasant?"

"It's in his name. I don't know who the bankroll is."

"I never use the joint, but I think I'll stroll over there now."

MORT USED a cab to travel ten blocks to the Golden Pheasant. It got its name from the imitation gold leaf of its decoration, and the customers were as phony as the gold leaf. Mort wondered why anybody like Mrs. Brownell, who definitely wasn't phony, despite her faults, could have spent any time at all in such a place. He went to the bar and ordered Scotch, which he detested.

The barman didn't ask him what brand. He automatically reached for a bottle on the back bar and poured a drink. The bottle bore the same label as that which had killed Tyler Fenwick. The barman reached for a soda bottle, and Mort asked for water. He put down the drink, hiding his distaste and said: "That's damn fine Scotch, pal. I haven't seen much of that in this man's town. Don't know where I could pick up a case or two, do you?"

The barman said he didn't know. He waited on another customer. Mort ordered another round and asked if he could see the manager. The barman pressed a button.

Presently a bald-headed man came out of a doorway and around the end of the bar. Mort watched the barman give the bald man a broad wink. The bald man came up to Mort and said: "I'm Rocky Romano. I own this place."

"Glad to meet you, Mr. Romano. I'm C.D. Mort. I like your Scotch. I like it enough to pay the right price if you could tell me where I can find some more."

"Why, Mr. Mort, as a lawyer you should know I can't handle that kind of thing! It would cost me my license if the liquor board ever found out."

Mort laughed in his face.

"You risked your license when you rang that stuff in here. As far as the liquor board's concerned, you're risking nothing by telling me who bootlegs. You ought to know that I can be trusted anyway."

Romano shook his head sorrowfully. "So sorry. I can't tell you because I don't know. I bought this Scotch legit."

Mort laughed in Romano's face and left the bar. He stopped at the first drugstore and called Blackie Jones.

"Have the Mayhew Agency find out who's flooding this town with Scotch. They've got it at the Golden Pheasant, and the same crowd sold Jock Martel some at one-fifty a case. It shouldn't be hard to find out. That kind of a deal takes a lot of dough—or credit."

Mort turned away from the booths, stopped as he noticed an open closet door disclosing two slot machines. Dust had accumulated on the slot machines. Mort walked from the drugstore and hailed a cab. He rode to the Lucky Club and ate a hearty meal.

He had just finished his second cup of coffee when Jack Bevans walked in. He sat down opposite Mort, his expression worried.

"I don't like this set-up, Mort. What you said's got me worried. I didn't want to admit it, but I've got to. You must know something or you wouldn't say there was danger I might get bumped off like Fenwick. I want to know."

"It was only a hunch, Jack, only a hunch."

"But you must have had some reason for having a hunch."

Mort put down his coffee cup, the contents emptied.

"I told you once, twice, and I'm telling you again—it's only a hunch. Are you going back downtown? Fine, you can drop me at the office."

Bevans' car was parked in the Lucky Club lot. The lot was well-lighted, but there were fringes of darkness. From one of the fringes came a flash of light, simultaneous with a sharp report. Bevans pitched forward. Mort flattened himself beside him. A bullet cracked the air behind his ear, as he did so. He lay quiet, not breathing. Bevans didn't seem to be breathing either.

There were no more shots.

Men came cautiously into the parking lot. Emboldened by the absence of further excitement, they advanced to the spot where the two men lay. Curtained from further attempts by the gunmen, Mort rose. He said: "Get an ambulance. This man's been hit!"

He struck a match. Bevans' coat had been torn at the right side and at the back. Blood streamed from an ugly rent. But Bevans was now breathing. Mort ripped away the cloth and applied his spare handkerchief to the wound. It was a gaping wound, irregular. Mort thought he could feel a bullet somewhere underneath. A squad car arrived, then the ambulance.

The interne said Bevans had only a matter of hours to live. Mort watched Bevans' prostrate body placed in the ambulance, then walked back into the Lucky Club. He phoned police headquarters, got Captain Merica on the wire. Merica already knew about the shooting.

"I want you to pick up everybody in the case," said Mort. "Have them all at the hospital. And I do mean Cornelius C. Newhall, too!"

AN HOUR later, standing at the end of the hospital corridor outside Bevans' door, Mort and Blackie watched the procession arrive. Jock Martel looked very much bored. Cornelius C. Newhall looked outraged. Shirley Brownell almost carried her mother as she came out of the elevator beside her.

"My God!" said Blackie. "They should keep her here! She looks as if she's going to have the snakes!"

Four other prominent Fairfax Heights residents arrived sheepishly, the four male guests who had attended Fenwick's party along with Jock Martel and Sylvia Farrell. The latter also appeared—in mourning. Quigley, the Fenwick gardener, was in working clothes.

Cornelius C. Newhall marched straight up to Mort.

"I presume you are behind this! I demand an explanation!"

Mort nodded to Merica, flanked by detectives.

"It's his party. Ask him."

Merica shook his head. "The whole case is in the D.A.'s lap. Here he is now."

A second elevator had disgorged the beefy figure of Harry Malone, district attorney. Malone spied Newhall's purple face, suppressed a belly laugh and approached Mort.

"Know what you're doing, C.D.? I hear a slug almost parted your own hair. Haw-haw!"

Mort watched frigidly as the district attorney had his laugh. "When the powers that be say we can see Bevans, we'll have it out in his room. Before we leave, you'll have your murderer."

Malone eyed Mort attentively. He shot a glance at Merica. Merica looked at Mort and shrugged. Five minutes later, a physician thrust his head outside Bevans' door.

"You can have ten minutes. I do not approve of this mass meeting in my patient's room, but the interests of justice seem to demand it. Make as little disturbance as possible, and remember—ten minutes!"

Jack Bevans' bed was adjusted so that he could see all who filed into the room. He was very pale. He smiled wanly to Mort.

"Sorry I didn't take your word for it, C.D."

Mort said: "It was only a hunch. I don't blame you for not listening."

Harry Malone said impatiently: "Let's hurry it up, C.D. We've got only ten minutes."

Mort nodded. "Folks, I wouldn't have had you brought here under normal circumstances. It's not my job to catch killers—but to defend them. In this case I've been retained by my client, Jack Bevans. He is not only a suspect in the Fenwick murder, but also a defendant in Mrs. Brownell's suit to cancel his contract to buy her home in Fairfax Heights. From the beginning I've felt that there was a definite connection between the two events.

"I hope even Mr. Newhall will forgive me if I say that I'm hardly a tyro in the practice of law. Every lawyer, in direct proportion to his experience, consciously or subconsciously seeks the cause behind effects. The effects may seem irrelevant, to have no importance whatever. Yet, when a lawyer sees an unusual effect, he looks for an unusual cause.

"For example, when I learned that Jock Martel had been buying Scotch at a hundred and fifty dollars a case, I thought this unusual because almost all of Jock's money is gone, and even his house in the Heights is mortgaged for all it's worth. So I wondered what unusual cause had brought about this unusual effect.

"Next, I noted that Mr. Martel was an enthusiastic partisan in the drive to prevent the sacred precincts of Fairfax Heights from being contaminated by Mr. Bevans. I wondered if this effect had the same cause as Mr. Martel's ability to buy hundred-and-fifty dollar Scotch. So I—"

"Listen, you," snapped Jock Martel, "I don't know what you're driving at, but if you're implying that I had anything to do with Tyler's murder, you're crazy!"

"Or me, either!" chimed in Newhall. "This is an outrage!"

"Quiet, please!" said the physician. "We must have no disturbance."

"And we haven't much time," said Harry Malone. "Get on with it, Mort. You can omit the speech as to how your great legal mind works."

Mort looked slightly hurt. "Really, Harry, to get my effect, I must explain its cause. Take, Mr. Newhall, here, the dean of the local bar, an elder in his church and a pillar of society. There is an ethical lawyer for you. He defines anything as ethical that gets him a fee. So he—"

"I will not stand here and tolerate such an unethical insult!" bellowed Newhall. "I'm leaving right now. You can't stop me—I'm a lawyer, and I know my rights!"

Malone stepped between Newhall and the door.

"Walk out of here, and, so help me, I'll have you jailed as a material witness." Newhall faltered. Malone turned to Mort and snapped: "Hurry it up, C.D."

Mort nodded obligingly. "As I was saying, I thought it unusual that Mr. Newhall should go into court with a case the success of which depended upon his making a liar out of me. I thought it even more absurd that he would attempt to make liars out of the officials at the Recorder's office, who were willing to testify that Mrs. Brownell was sober when she left there. I decided that this was because Mr. Newhall mistakenly thought he had a chance to win his case.

"The recording time on Mrs. Brownell's receipt indicated that she had left there one hour and sixteen minutes before she entered my office. The employees at the Golden Pheasant were prepared to testify that Mrs. Brownell spent an hour of the intervening time in that establishment and that she was under the influence of intoxicating liquor when she left it in company with Bevans. That set of facts explains why Mr. Newhall was willing to take such a case— he thought the evidence was in his favor.

"However, someone slipped. The brain behind the scheme forgot that two time systems are extant in our state—Eastern Standard war time as adopted by the city council and Central Standard war time as adopted by our state legislature. The County Courthouse is operated as a subdivision of the state—therefore it operates on the slower time. There's an hour's difference. So, if the receipt to Mrs. Brownell shows anything at all, it shows that the Golden Pheasant employees are liars. She left the courthouse at nine-thirty-one "slow" time or ten-thirty-one "fast" time, giving her sixteen minutes to get to my office and proving she couldn't possibly have been getting drunk at that time."

"**BY JOVE!**" exclaimed Newhall. "That's true! I never thought of that. This time conflict has me mixed up all the time!"

"I'll take your professional word for that," said Mort graciously. "You were misled by someone who assumed that a clerk at the Recorder's office had made a mistake and who sought to capitalize on it."

"Tyler Fenwick?" asked Newhall. "He was the man who did all of the talking!"

"No. You were misled by the man behind Fenwick. I refer to Jock Martel."

"You're crazy!" Martel snapped. "I had nothing to do with these murders!"

"But the evidence is against you. You bought a brand of Scotch that you couldn't afford. The same brand is on sale at the Golden Pheasant, where the waiters and barmen were prepared to perjure themselves to help keep Jack Bevans out of Fairfax Heights. Yes, Jock, you were behind Tyler Fenwick, using him as a pawn in the game. It's too bad for him—and you—that he found it out!"

Perspiration streamed down Martel's temples.

"You can't prove anything!"

"Oh, yes, I can. I can prove a fact which I overlooked until I visited a drugstore tonight. Thanks to Mr. Malone, here, the heat has been on slot machines for months. I was reminded of this when I saw a couple of slots tucked away in a closet and covered with dust. So I decided that my client, Mr. Bevans, was not nearly so prosperous as he was reputed to be, not nearly rich enough to buy a house for seventy-five thousand dollars.

"I also decided that if my client could not operate slot machines, he would be engaging in some other activity, preferably one in no way connected with manual labor.

Flooding the city with black-market Scotch would be right in his line. But that would take capital. He would have to find a backer. Now, I asked myself, what is the best way to interest backers?

"The best way is to prove one's prosperity. One way to do that is to contract to buy a seventy-five-thousand-dollar house. Everybody hears about it—everybody is impressed. Everybody is willing to lend you money. So I decided that Jack Bevans had signed the contract with Mrs. Brownell, binding him to pay a fabulous price for her house, solely to build up his credit.

"Naturally he wouldn't want to go through with such a contract. So he secured the services of Jock Martel, who needed both money and Scotch. Martel stirred up an anti-Bevan sentiment in Fairfax Heights, and Mrs. Brownell was induced to start a suit to cancel her contract. Bevans was then in a position to renounce it on the ground that she had already disaffirmed it. Legally he could back out of the deal without any cost greater than negligible attorney fees and a few crumbs to Jock Martel.

"But last night Martel attended Fenwick's party, bringing enough of his Scotch to put himself in such a condition that he told the truth. Fenwick contacted Bevans, threatened to expose the whole scheme and have Mrs. Brownell drop her case. Bevans then went out to Fenwick's place, parking discreetly away from the drive. He tried to reason with Fenwick, but Fenwick had too much money to be bought. So Bevans lost his head and killed him. Miss Brownell almost caught him, but he ducked, later coming into the drive in his car to establish an alibi."

In his bed, Bevans lay nearly paralyzed. He managed to scream: "My own lawyer! I hired you to defend me! You've no right to do this! You're selling out your own client!"

Mort eyed him coldly. "No, Jack. I'm not selling you out. You sold me out. I'd have kept my mouth closed if you hadn't. When I went out to the Lucky Club I felt like a condemned man. I knew you were guilty of murder. Yet I had to go through with defending you. But you changed all that when you led me out into the parking lot so that your paid gunman could shoot me just like a fish in a barrel!"

"Shoot you? Why, I'm the guy who got shot!"

"That's all that saved me. That first shot was aimed low, to make me think I wasn't the target. The second shot was to get me. But the first one struck the wall around the parking lot a glancing blow and ricocheted, hitting you in the side." Mort turned on the physician.

"Am I right in saying that the bullet was smashed, that it was almost spent when it struck Bevans? Am I also right when I say the wound was jagged because the bullet was distorted, but that it was only a harmless, superficial wound?"

The physician nodded.

"Absolutely, Mr. Mort. But you'll have to go now. The time's up."

"Just a minute," begged Malone. "Why did Bevans try to have you killed, C.D.?"

"The electronic record in my office would have cinched the Brownell case for him. He learned only today that I have a record of the entire conference when Mrs. Brownell signed the contract. He planned to put me out of the way so he could take care of the record without interference."

"But he didn't have to win it! He could have dropped out of the case regardless of the evidence."

"Not without opening my eyes. I'd have seen through his game in a flash, and he knew it."

Malone whistled. "That's the first time I ever heard of a client trying to kill his lawyer to stop him from winning his case!"

Mort sighed wearily. "I'll protect myself from other lawyers if only God will protect me from my clients!"

MURDER UNDER FOOT

"CORPUS DELICTI" MORT WAS
NOW ON THE OTHER SIDE OF
THE FENCE—PROSECUTING HIS
FRIENDS AND FORMER CLIENTS.
BUT TWO-WAY BLACKMAIL, SOME
FAST SHOOTING, AND A VERY
DEAD DRUNK CONVINCED HIM
THAT HE WASN'T CUT OUT TO BE
A CITY SOLICITOR, AND HE FREE-
LANCED BACK TO TRAP A VERY
SURPRISED KILLER.

CHAPTER ONE
DEAD DRUNK

THE MUNICIPAL courtroom was packed.

Judge Harmon glowered upon the unprecedented throng, apparently racking his brain for an excuse to clear the room. For the first time in his twenty years as a municipal judge, he was finding his court the center of attraction. During those years thousands of misdemeanor cases had passed unnoticed through his fingers, now even the most negligible case attracted newspaper reporters en masse.

Judge Harmon appreciated the reason for this, and he resented him. He could not enjoy the unwanted popularity of his courtroom because he realized his own role was merely that of a supernumerary. The star of the case, the drawing card that had brought the unprecedented audience, was the acting city solicitor, Clarence Darrow Mort.

"Corpus Delicti" Mort they called him around the criminal courts building, where he reigned supreme. Defender of more than a hundred alleged murderers, Mort had never lost one of them to the vengeance of the law. Always the champion of the accused, now, as prosecutor for the city, he found his role reversed.

Harry Carter, the regular city solicitor, had suggested the appointment as a gag. The mayor had been amused by the idea and had phoned Mort, tongue in cheek. He had been the most surprised man in the city when Mort, never batting an eye, had replied that it would be a great pleasure and honor to act as city solicitor while Harry Carter took his two weeks' vacation.

So for the past week Judge Harmon's courtroom had been mobbed by curious onlookers intrigued by the spectacle of the great criminal lawyer acting in the shoes of a prosecutor of crime. In a number of cases already Mort had found himself prosecuting for small misdemeanors men whom he had formerly defended on much more serious charges. If the defendants were embarrassed, Mort was not. He was taking his new part in his stride.

This morning, however, the audience waited and watched in almost unendurable suspense. There had been a vice raid the night before, and among those caught in the net was Madam Malone, proprietress of a super de luxe establishment in which gentlemen might take a chance. Always a gambler, Mort had been one of the place's best patrons, and it was well known that Madam Malone regarded him as one of her best, if not her best friend.

"Five will get you ten," whispered Jack Woods, reporter for the *Citizen,* "that you can fry an egg on Mort's face when they bring her in."

Petie Cardoza, of the *Dispatch,* scoffed. "You don't know Mort if that's what you think. He'll never bat an eye. You watch."

Jack Woods, in common with a hundred others within the room, watched. The bailiff gaveled unecessarily for order.

"Case Number 23765, The City of Riverton vs. Sadie Q. Malone."

At his signal, a deputy opened a door, and Madam Malone swept in. She was a woman of uncertain age, but there could be no doubt about her weight which must have been in excess of two hundred and twenty-five pounds. The weight of her diamonds made a tangible increase.

Madam Malone looked hard at Mort, and Mort seemed to be very much interested in shuffling the papers on his table. He did not look up as Madam Malone raised her right hand and took the oath. She then climbed the steps to the witness chair, and it creaked as she rested her weight in it.

The bailiff read the charge, one of operating a gambling establishment in violation of a municipal ordinance to the contrary. Madam Malone pleaded not guilty, and the preliminary examination was under way. Mort cleared his throat. "You will state your name, please."

Madam Malone glared at her best customer. The glare clearly indicated that she thought the supplying of such common knowledge was superfluous. But she said: "Sadie Q. Malone."

Still busy with his papers, Mort asked: "Where is your place of business?"

It was too much for Madam Malone. She snorted: "Well, you ought to know—you've been there often enough!"

Mort said patiently: "I know I have, but the judge hasn't—please answer the question."

The room became a bedlam. Judge Harmon was paralyzed with laughter and powerless to restore order. The bailiff and his deputy were holding their sides. The newspaper reporters had fled howling to their phones. Even Madam Malone was chuckling in her chair. The only straight face in the room belonged to Mort.

He still seemed intrigued by his papers.

"Please answer the question, Madam Malone," he repeated, as the uproar subsided.

"Down, Blackie!" Mort snapped. "You're too big a target as it is. Miss Talbott, you lie flat on the floor!"

Madam Malone, a twinkle in her eye, said: "Same old stand, C.D. Corner of Cherry and Chestnut."

"Are you aware that the operation of a gambling establishment is contrary to Ordinance Number 1206 of this city and that a fine of one hundred dollars is imposed on any person found guilty of such a violation?"

"One hundred dollars?" Madam Malone's mouth hung open. "Are you telling me that a century is all the rap I can take on this beef?"

"A hundred dollars, madam, is the maximum penalty."

"Well, why didn't somebody tell me? If I'd known that's all the beef amounted to, I'd have sent one of my girls down to square it!"

Mort's brows lifted. "Haven't you sought legal advice in this case?"

"I should say not! You're the only mouthpiece I'd hire, C.D., and you're working for the law right now. I figured on hiring you to defend me as soon as the regular city solicitor got back on the job! But since the beef's only a century, I think I'll pay it. You'd want that much to blow your nose!"

Mort was again busy with his papers.

"Very well, madam. You will enter your plea with the clerk and pay such fine as the Court may direct."

Judge Harmon hid his grin with the back of his hand, said the fine would be a hundred and costs, and in a matter of a minute Sadie Q. Malone had flounced out of the room. The next case was called. It was a traffic case.

THE BAILIFF announced: "Case Number 23766, the City of Riverton vs. Mary Jorg." Ears pricked up as the accused entered the room accompanied by her attorney. This was owing in no part to the attorney, who was a wizened little party named Jerry Wales. Jerry was a small-time criminal lawyer sustained only through his desperate cooperation with a bail bond broker named Jack Chester. Chester gave Wales routine petty cases which even he could not mess up, and every habitue of the courtroom had come to take Wales as a matter of course.

But his client, Mary Jorg, was definitely not matter of course. A striking brunette, she looked as out of place as a pickpocket at a Rotarian lunch. However, she strode coolly before the court, seemingly quite at home and at ease.

Even Mort's brows were lifted in wondrous appraisal. He was not one to be impressed by expensive clothes, but he had long ago learned to distinguish between a woman dressed up to her usual par and a woman simply dressed up. This girl wore her obviously expensive clothes in a manner which indicated that she had never worn any other kind. Mort studied her with interest.

The bailiff read the charge. Mary Jorg, said the traffic patrolman's affidavit, had driven her Cadillac convertible car at a speed of thirty-five miles in a closely-built up business district in which the lawful limit was only twenty-five. Judge Harmon frowned. Because of a local effort to reduce traffic accidents, a jail sentence of one day had been imposed in addition to the usual fine. Judge Harmon was a man of rigid principles ill disposed toward granting favors to special persons. But it was plain he did not care to send the lovely defendant to jail.

"How do you plead," demanded the bailiff, "guilty or not guilty?"

Before Mary Jorg could reply, Jerry Wales popped to his feet. "May we have five minutes' recess, Your Honor? I'm waiting for a witness."

Judge Harmon jumped at a chance to put off an unpleasant duty. He nodded, ordered the recess and left the bench. Immediately Jerry Wales walked past Mort, saying out of the side of his mouth: "Meet me in the press room. Just this once, Mort—please!"

Mort waited two minutes, then walked into the press room. It was deserted save for Wales. "Well?"

The little shyster was almost tearful. "C.D., I know you can't be fixed. But please, *please* give me a break! There's five hundred in it for me if I beat this case. Cripes, C.D., think what I can do with five bills! I owe everybody—this would give me a breather. Boy, how I need it!"

Mort eyed him sternly. "You're breaking my heart. Who do you take me for, expecting me to believe anybody'd pay you half a grand for beating a ten-and-costs rap with a day in the clink?"

"Honest, C.D., that's on the level! The gal's got it, and she'll give it to me if only I spring her out of here without that day. That's what's eating her, not the ten and costs!"

Mort's brows drew severely together. "Then let's fling her into jail. Maybe that'll teach her to drive slower."

Bona fide tears welled in Wales' eyes. "You can't do this to me, C.D.! Remember the old days. We were pals then. For old times' sake, C.D., give me this one break, and I'll never ask another. Why I'll even pay you that fifty I owe you!" His face became horrified then, as he saw Mort's eyes, and he added desperately: "No, C.D., I didn't mean that! I wasn't tryin' to make a fix! I just meant I'd appreciate your giving me this break!"

Mort turned on his heel and walked back into the room. Wales followed him in dire dejection. He slumped at the defense table, and when his attractive client attempted to query him, he waved a hand at her and looked away. Judge Harmon returned to the bench. The bailiff called the room to order.

"Are you ready to proceed, Mr. Mort?" asked the judge.

Mort rose solemnly. "Your Honor, I've learned from a conversation with the arresting officer, Patrolman McCoy, that there are certain extenuating circumstances in this case. The accused, Miss Jorg, at the time she was speeding, was rushing to the hospital to see her dying mother. With the Court's approval, I recommend that the charges against her be dropped."

Judge Harmon eyed Mort speculatively. He regarded Patrolman McCoy, who stood by open-mouthed. "Is this true, Officer?"

Mort gave Patrolman McCoy a hard look. McCoy gulped. Mort had never seen the man before in his life, but McCoy knew his place. The city solicitor was in control of the case. A mere traffic cop could only nod and acquiesce. So McCoy nodded. "Yes, Your Honor. That's what she was doin', goin' to the hospital."

"Was her mother there? Did you check?" McCoy whitened. "Yes, Your Honor, I checked."

Judge Harmon shrugged. "Case dismissed. Next case."

MORT STUDIOUSLY avoided Jerry Wales' eye, but out of the corner of his own eye he saw that the lawyer was jubilant. He shooed his client from the room, and Mort noted that Mary Jorg also was regarding him appreciatively. Mort chuckled to himself. He knew that Judge Harmon was more grateful than anyone else. Mary Jorg was the first woman arrested since the traffic drive had started, and the judge would have been forced to establish a precedent. Mort guessed that in the future the city police would be instructed to make no more arrests of women. At any rate, he was glad to be able to gain a windfall for Jerry.

The day dragged on. At five in the afternoon court was adjourned, and Mort was in a state of near exhaustion. Petie Cardoza and Jack Woods had stuck with him all day, phoning their reports to their respective papers. They met Mort as he left the room.

"I'll buy," said Petie. "Boy, what a beating you've taken today! And all for the lousy ten bucks salary of a city solicitor. What's come over you? Why five hundred a day's always been your rock-bottom fee!"

Mort sighed. "Well, Petie, it's like this. The novelty of being on the other side of the fence appeals to me. But mainly I'm learning something."

Jack Woods laughed incredulously. "You're kidding! You know all there is in the book backwards."

"That's just what I've been afraid of lately—that I know it backwards. A criminal lawyer gets a sort of astigmatism after so many years of practice. He sees a case only from the rear end, from behind the eight-ball his client's got in front of him. He gets so he loses his perspective. That's why criminal lawyers so often slip. Take Jerry Wales."

Jack Woods scoffed. "You take him. He's not even a has-been, he's a never-wuzzer."

Mort eyed the reporter gravely. Then he turned to Petie Cardoza. "Tell him, Petie. You remember when."

Petie eyed his colleague narrowly. "Believe it or not, Jack, time was when Jerry Wales was the top criminal lawyer of this man's town!"

Jack's eyes widened. "You're kidding!"

"Nope. Fifteen years ago, Jerry had it. But all of a sudden his luck changed. It seemed a jury convicted a guy just on the ground that Jerry was his lawyer. After that the poor guy'd have starved but for Jack Chester."

"Good Lord—that seems incredible!"

"But true," said Mort. "Come along, only I'll buy. Believe me, I can use a double-shot or two."

He had downed his fourth at Luigi's when a barman told him he was wanted on the phone. That would be his partner, Blackie Jones, he decided. Blackie was holding the fort at his office during his stint as city solicitor.

But it wasn't Blackie. It was Madam Malone. "There's a drunk in my kitchen," she said tersely. "He's been bothering me for the last half hour. He wants five grand."

"For what?"

"For information."

"What kind of information?"

"It's not for telling on the phone. I want you to come out. I want the dope this punk's got, but not for five grand. Make a cheaper deal, and it'll be worth your while."

"But Sadie, I'm in no position to take up private practice. Have you forgotten that I'm acting city solicitor?"

"Hell, no. But you can make an exception this once."

"Tell you what I'll do. I'll send Blackie."

"Nix. The big guy's a sweet kid, but not up to handling this guy in my kitchen."

"By the way, who is he?"

"Jerry Wales."

"Oh." Mort reflected. Then he said: "Take it easy. I'll get out in due course."

He went back to his drinking companions and ordered another round. By this time they were beyond taking notice of the fact that he skipped his own drink. After a decent and disarming interval he excused himself. His car was parked in the city building lot, but he took a cab. After all, somebody might make something of it if his own car were spotted at Madam Malone's the same day he had had her arrested.

He instructed the driver to pull into the alley at the rear of the house. When he alighted, he climbed the steps of the enclosed back porch and rang a bell. Presently Madam Malone appeared in person. "You finally got here!" she groaned. "I'm afraid you're too late. Jerry's passed out cold."

Mort entered the kitchen. Jerry Wales was slumped over the table. Mort eased him back gently, then he immediately let the lawyer fall forward. Madam Malone eyed him strangely. "The way you look—what's up?"

"Jerry isn't drunk this time, Sadie. He's dead. One of your kitchen knives is buried in his chest."

CHAPTER TWO
MAN'S BEST FRIEND
IS HIS MURDER

MORT KNEW where to find a phone, and he found it. He called Headquarters. Then he turned to find Madam Malone, pale behind him. "This'll ruin me, C.D.! The scandal of a murder in the house will put me right out of business! You've simply got to crack the case before the cops spread it all over the papers and make a nine-days' wonder out of it!"

Mort said: "All right. Why don't you confess?"

Sadie Malone took a step backwards. "C.D., you're kidding!"

"I know I am, but the cops won't be when they ask the same question. Jerry was here to shake you down for five grand. You lost your temper, seized a kitchen knife and let him have it. Then you call me, pretend he's still alive and invite me out to discover the body."

"You know that's preposterous!"

"Not to a lot of people. A lot of people will think a woman in your racket is capable of anything. Enough of them may make the jury."

"Mort, I'm retaining you right now. Write your own ticket—but find the right guy and hang this one on him!"

Mort hesitated, then said: "It's a deal."

"Fine! What'll I do now?"

"Pay me a five-grand retainer."

What! Why, I haven't got that much money in the bank!"

"I believe you. But you've got ten times that in a sock somewhere. Get it."

Sadie Malone cursed softly, then left the room. Mort was contemplating the corpse in the kitchen when she returned and laid down ten five hundred-dollar bills. Mort pocketed them absently, then said: "All right, let's have it."

"I can't give you much. Jerry came here a while ago pretty well stung and asked for a private little talk. First off he tells me he knows who's been putting the bite on me. So—"

"Back up a minute! So somebody's been shaking you down—besides the cops, I mean."

"And plenty! First it was a grand, then a grand and a half, finally the bite was two at a crack. All told I've paid out about fifteen in the past year."

"For what?"

"For my daughter."

"Your *what?*"

"You heard me. Not many folks in the world know I was ever even married. A lot fewer ever heard of my daughter. I've kept her away in a swell school. She never comes to Riverton. She thinks I'm a buyer for a department store always on the road. She'd hate my guts if she ever found out the truth. I couldn't stand that, and this wise guy knows it."

"You mean the lad who's collected the fifteen grand?"

"Yes. Don't think I haven't done my best to nail him down. He phones from a different spot every time, and every time I've got to leave the dough at a different place. He's cagy. I hired the Mayhew Detective Agency to catch him, but he wouldn't touch the dough. He called me up and gave me hell and said the next time I pulled that one the ante would double."

"Sadie, I'm really surprised at you."

She wiped a tear from each eye. "You don't understand. You've never been a mother."

"Check on that one, Sadie. So Jerry walks in and tells you he knows who's shaking you down?"

"Yes. When he said he had to have the five bills I stalled him. I said I didn't keep that kind of dough in the house at this hour of the night and he'd have to wait. So I left him and phoned you right away. I figured you could handle him."

"You didn't come back?"

"Not until I let you in."

"You keep this door locked, don't you?"

"Of course. But doors don't generally stop killers."

"Anybody inside could have done it."

"They'd have had to get by me in the hallway. That's out. The job was done by somebody using the back door."

Mort sighed. "You might as well give me all the facts. It's a cinch that whoever's been collecting from you has crossed your path or your daughter's some time or other. Think back. Whom do you know who would have knowledge of your daughter?"

"Nobody. That is, nobody who could connect Mary Jorg with me."

"*What?*" Mort shouted. He brought his voice down, as Sadie eyed him with puzzlement. "Do you mean that you didn't see Mary Jorg today and she didn't see you?"

Sadie paled slightly. "You're kidding! I couldn't have seen her today. She's at Carlton College, five hundred miles from here."

"The devil she is! She was in Riverton this morning and in municipal court on a traffic charge. Her case came right after yours. It's incredible that you could have missed seeing each other."

"Mort, are you on the level?" She studied him, then said: "Well, I don't know how it happened, but I didn't see Mary. I hope to God she didn't see me."

MORT REFLECTED. "Jerry Wales was her lawyer. He said she'd offered him five hundred if he'd beat the jail rap. I fronted for him, and she did. I think I'm beginning to understand why it was worth that kind of dough for the girl to walk out of court. She didn't want a conviction and a jail sentence to make the papers where you'd see it. She didn't want you to know she was in Riverton."

Sadie sat down hard on a kitchen chair.

"You think she knows?"

"I'd make a book on it."

"But who would tell her?"

"The same blackmailer that's been collecting from you. He could work it both ways—make her pay off to avoid having the truth get out at that college."

"But she never told me…"

"If she loved you she wouldn't. She'd keep the secret to herself to avoid hurting you. My guess is that she told Jerry Wales her real reason for wanting to beat the jail rap this morning. So Jerry worked fast today and found out who was pulling the blackmail. He had more racket connections than anyone in town."

Sadie was in tears. "Think of what that poor child has been going through for her no-account mother!"

"Skip the soap opera," said Mort. "We've got murder underfoot. Here's the law now."

Mort swore to himself as he recognized Lieutenant Garrett through the door window. Garrett was a newly promoted homicide detective, and he was perpetually attempting to cover himself with glory. Mort had no objection to this laudable ambition, but he did dislike Garrett's tendency to push people aside in his mad rush for success. Mort had no intention of being pushed aside. He opened the door and faced Garrett.

"You dope!" said Garrett. "Now your fingerprints are all over the doorknob!"

"And yours are going to be all over the floor if you don't watch your tongue!" Mort snapped. "When did the last killer in this man's town leave his prints anywhere anyway?"

Garrett maintained his attitude of severe disgust. "We never know when somebody will slip and do it. A fat chance we got if this is the time." He crossed to Wales and gave him a professional stare. "Well, well, I always knew the little shyster would wind up behind the eight-ball!"

Mort took a position in front of the detective.

"Listen, you flatfooted lame-brain, you're talking about a member of the bar! He might not have been an ornament to it, but he had more brains than all the homicide dicks between here and the Suez Canal. What if he was a shyster? That's just the name a lawyer gets for not being successful. If they had a name for cops of the same caliber, you'd be it!"

Garrett reddened, the more so because a pair of plain-clothesmen had followed him into the kitchen and they showed their disappointment at their superior's failure to cope with Mort in a duel of invective.

"I haven't got time to argue with you now," Garrett said. He whirled on Sadie. "So you even got your lawyer on the job before you called Headquarters? Are you going to sign a confession, or are we going to have to fry you the hard way?"

Sadie put her hands on her hips. "Button your lip, you small-time chiseler. The last time I remember you, you were palming apples off a fruit stand in front of my place on Veesie Street and coming to my back door at nights for sugar. Why, you—"

"Control yourself," Mort interrupted. "There's no reason why either of us should let this frustrated pickpocket get our goat. Now, see here, Garrett, it was like this...."

In a few minutes Mort handed the detective a story of truths and half-truths. The truth was when he told Garrett of his call from Sadie, of her desire to have an important conference with him. The half-truths were involved in his glossing over the motive for the conference as "confidential affairs of my client."

"What are you giving me?" Garrett glowered. "You can't hold out on me like that. What was this little punk doing here? Don't tell me he'd come to Sadie's back door for a hand-out."

"Boy," said one of the plainclothesmen, "I'll say he didn't! Look at this! Five centuries! Where'd the little runt ever get that kind of dough?"

Garrett's eyes widened as he saw the bills. He snatched them from the detective's hands, spun on Mort.

"Did you give him these? What for?"

"One question at a time, you inhibited counterfeiter. The answer to the first question is no, and the answer to the second is therefore superfluous."

"Well, you know where he got the dough. Let's have it."

"O.K. My guess is that Jerry must have been working for the police on the side. They're the only people I know of who have a license to steal."

Garrett reddened. "I'll take you downtown, and then you'll answer!"

Mort played his trump card. "You'll take me downtown! Why, you insufferable lout, I'll report this to the mayor! Imagine, threatening to arrest the city solicitor!"

Garrett rocked on his heels. He was so accustomed, like all other detectives on the city force, to regarding Mort as the champion of the accused, the defender of the suspect, that he had completely forgotten that the lawyer was temporarily a prosecuting attorney and in point of fact a higher ranking law enforcement officer than himself. To drag Mort in for interfering with his investigation of a crime would be even more preposterous than dragging in the chief of police for the same offense.

Mort took advantage of triumph. "It is not my official duty to dabble with detecting," he said grandly. "That is the prerogative of lesser minds. When you have made your investigation, Garrett, bring me your guesses, however ridiculous."

With that, Mort strode from the kitchen and across the back porch, his effect marred only slightly as he stumbled over a case of empty beer bottles.

HE WALKED out the alley and emerged into the street. A neon sign proclaimed that a drugstore was a half-block away. Mort entered the drugstore and made two calls. The first was to the Mayhew Detective Agency. Mort instructed the agency to find Mary Jorg at all costs, either in Riverton or at Carlton College. He referred the agency to the police files for her license plate number, gave a brief description.

He chuckled as he dialed his second call, to the Acme Shooting Galleries. He knew that his junior partner, Blackie Jones, would be there, wasting good ammunition in a futile attempt to become an expert pistol shot. It amused him that six-foot-seven Blackie, easily capable of tossing a wrestler back into a ring, should try so desperately and fail so wretchedly to make even a fair score with a little .22-caliber target pistol.

This was especially gratifying to Mort, standing only a few inches over five feet in height, who could crack a ninety any day of the week with an Army .45. It was poetic justice he felt, and he gloated whenever the opportunity arose.

"Have you hit a bull's-eye yet?" he asked Blackie, when the youth answered the phone. He could almost hear Blackie gnashing his teeth.

"You aren't that much interested in my pistol shooting. What's up? Have the cops raided your pal Sadie again? Sorry I missed the burlesque show this morning—everybody says your low comedy even got a laugh from pickle-puss Harmon!"

"The cops are at Sadie's again," said Mort gravely. "Only this time it isn't the vice squad—it's homicide. Somebody knifed Jerry Wales in her kitchen."

"What! Now, who would want to rub out that little bum?"

"I don't know who would want to murder our treasured colleague," Mort chastened him, "but I intend to find out. I've already sicked the Mayhew Detective Agency on him.

Lieutenant Garrett's assigned to the case, and he couldn't find a fish in a barrel. There're angles to this that'll bear watching."

"So! Where do I come in?"

"I want you to do a job on Jack Chester, the bail bond shark. He gave Jerry Wales desk room in a dark corner of his office. All of Jerry's records should be there—if he left any records. The odds are nothing will turn up, but we'll play the long shot. I'm counting on you to go through Jerry's desk."

"Oh, you are, are you? What do you think I am in this firm, vice-president in charge of breaking and entering? If you want anything out of Jack Chester's office, steal it yourself!"

"You know I'd get caught, at my age. Hurry it up, now— even Garrett will think of visiting Chester's rooms for a look into that desk. Besides, you can cover up. Phone Chester and tell him you want to meet him at his office. Then if anybody walks in on you, you can say you found the door open and just wandered in. By the time Chester gets there from his place out in Bexley you should be through with your job. It's a cinch."

Mort didn't wait for comment. He hung up, went outside and waited for a cab. He didn't have long to wait, for Madam Malone's establishment drew cabs like flies. He gave the driver his office address. Until the Mayhew Agency reported or Blackie struck pay dirt in Jerry's desk, he could only wait. At least, he thought so.

"May I have a word with you, Mr. Mort?" the young man said, as Mort crossed the sidewalk to enter his office building. Mort halted. For a moment he couldn't place the callow face, then he remembered. Henry Allen, Jr., was a newcomer in the city's night life, but when he appeared, he was pointed out. His father, Henry Allen, Sr., was the city's richest manufacturer, but he had kept tight reins on his only son and heir. It was rumored that young Henry's only source of income was the modest salary that he rated as a comparatively humble employee in one of his father's factories. But lately Henry had been giving a lie to the rumor. Casual observers guessed that his gambling losses totaled several times the stipend his father reputedly paid him.

"Certainly," said Mort. "Just a minute, and the night man will let us in. You're Henry Allen, I believe?"

Allen nodded. "It's very important, Mr. Mort. I can hardly wait to talk to you."

But Mort made him wait when he had ushered him into his private office. Allen didn't want a drink, but Mort did, and when he poured one for his guest, there was no refusal. When Mort had swallowed his drink, he put down the glass and said: "All right, son, what's on your mind?"

"It's Mary—Mary Jorg. You met her today in municipal court. Do you remember?"

"I remember."

"Well, I'm going to marry her."

"My congratulations."

"It's not so simple, Mr. Mort. You know about my father, I suppose."

"Yes, I've read about him."

"Oh, I don't mean do you know about all his factories and stuff. I mean, do you know about his private life, how he's handled me?"

"It seems I've heard a little something about your father being pretty straight-laced and holding you down pretty carefully. But when I saw you making the hot spots lately I discounted that story."

"You needn't. It's the truth, every bit of it. You see, Mr. Mort, Dad has a theory that I mustn't be spoiled. That's why he makes me spend my time learning a lot of dumb jobs in his factories. He thinks he's starting me from the ground up and letting me learn the business from every angle. By confining me to the salary I make, he figured he'd keep me from cutting up any with wine, women and song."

"But you fooled him, hey?"

"Well, if you mean, did I take it lying down, I didn't. I wouldn't be my father's son if I didn't know how to pick up some dough. I've got plenty of inside information on the stock in a lot of the companies Dad has his fingers in, so I started playing the market. That's why you've been seeing me around."

"That's interesting, but it doesn't tell me what all this has to do with Mary Jorg."

"I'm coming to that. I wanted you to understand how excessively respectable the old man is. I don't hesitate to cross him on his insistence that I live on my pitiable salary, but I don't want to fight with him over the girl I marry."

"Why should you?"

"Because I'm afraid he'll find out about Mary. Oh, he knows her already, and he thinks she's swell. But he doesn't know the truth about her. If he ever does, he'll disinherit me if I ever speak to her again."

"My goodness, what's the awful truth? Does she eat with her knife?"

"This is serious with me, Mr. Mort. I'm willing to pay you any fee you ask if you'll only keep my father from finding out who Mary really is. Before I tell you, I want your word that you'll never expose her real identity."

"You have my word."

"Well, then, her mother's Madam Malone!"

ALLEN SAT back for an effect which he did not get. Mort eyed him calmly.

"Oh, I knew that. I thought you were going to tell me something important."

"Why, Mr. Mort, surely you understand! Madam Malone is—"

"One of my best friends," Mort finished. "Of course I can picture your father's horror at having his only son lawfully wedded to the daughter of a lady so notorious. However, if the girl's half-way as good as her mother, you're getting the best of the deal."

"I know that, Mr. Mort. I'm terribly in love with Mary. I'd marry her regardless, but if there's any way to stop the truth from getting out, I'll pay any price to keep it that way!"

"What makes you think the truth will get out?"

"Somebody's been blackmailing Mary. Somebody called her up and told her about Madam Malone. At first she refused to believe it, but she came to Riverton and managed to see her mother without being seen. The blackmailer was clever. As soon as he knew Mary was convinced, he began to demand money for silence. Finally it got so she had hardly enough money to stay in school."

"You're telling me a lot. When are you going to tell me why she was in Riverton today?"

"She came here last night. She came to see me. I was so tied up at the factory that I couldn't get away. Mary's done it several times. She stays with Helen Talbott, a cousin of mine. It was through Helen that I met Mary—they both go to Carlton. I can count on Helen."

"Are you telling me she knows about Madam Malone?"

"Yes, but I repeat that she can be trusted. She's Mary's best friend. Why, she's the one that put up the five hundred today to pay Mary's lawyer in that traffic case. Mary wouldn't take the money from me."

"Now that such an interesting subject has come up, why was it worth five bills for Mary Jorg to beat a traffic rap?"

"It wasn't the rap she was afraid of, it was the publicity. You see, I happened to know that Judge Harmon had committed himself to making no exceptions for women in this traffic safety drive. He was at Dad's house last night and said if a woman was found guilty in his court she'd go to jail for a day just like a man. So I knew what Dad would think if Mary made the papers as the first woman to go to jail in the new safety drive. I wanted to pay for a lawyer myself, but she wouldn't take the money from me. So Helen went to her rescue."

"How'd you come to pick on Jerry Wales?"

"Jack Chester, the bail bond man, recommended him. He said this Wales was a pal of yours and could get you to do a favor for him if the price was right."

Mort stood up. "Are you trying to tell me that Wales was supposed to have spent some of that five hundred fixing me?"

Allen seemed startled. "Why, I—er, I didn't think much about it. After all, you *did* let Mary walk out without even paying a fine!"

Mort slapped his jaw with the palms of his hands. "So help me, I'll never learn! I try to do a favor for a broken-down colleague, and what do I get out of it? The assumption that I'm a crook. If there's anything that'll lead a man to his downfall, it's a kind heart."

"Really, Mr. Mort, I didn't think you'd take it like that! After all, you must know you've something of a reputation as a shrewd operator. That's why I've come to you now. I figured that if anybody knew how to deal with a black-mailer, you would."

Mort sat back into his chair and chuckled resignedly to himself. "Forget it, son. I'd momentarily forgotten that a criminal lawyer is supposed to be the cheapest kind of crook. And naturally, if you want to catch a crook, you hire one to catch him. Well, let's get busy. But first I want to talk to Mary Jorg."

Allen brightened. "Fine, I'll take you right to her!"

Mort rose. The phone rang. He answered it. It was Ed Snyder reporting for the Mayhew Detective Agency.

"We've located the Jorg girl. Quick work, if I do say it. She's right here in town staying with—"

"Helen Talbott," Mort finished. "I'm going out to talk to her now. Thanks a lot, and send me your bill."

He hung up. The phone rang again as he went out the door, but he let it go. He knew he had rankled Snyder. Snyder would want to sound off. Well, he would let him burn.

CHAPTER THREE
KILLER IN THE CORNER

HELEN TALBOTT lived with her mother in a Washington Road apartment. She eyed Mort with mild curiosity, then discreetly excused herself, saying she would send Mary Jorg into the sitting room. It was one of those rooms where a guest has to decide which chairs are to be sat upon. Mort selected one that looked substantial enough for his hundred and thirty pounds and subsided uneasily.

He got up a second later when Mary Jorg came into the room. She looked even more attractive than she had that morning. Now that Mort knew who her mother was, he could see a certain resemblance. He wondered if Madam Malone had been that slim at her daughter's age, and if Mary would eventually be as fat as her mother. It had been this speculation about girls turning out to look like their mothers that had kept Mort a bachelor all these years.

"Hank's told you everything, I suppose," Mary Jorg said after the introduction.

Mort nodded. "With perhaps some minor omissions. That's why I wanted to talk to you. When did you first find out who your mother really was?"

"About a year ago. This man called me up and told me. Apparently he had quite a lot of fun doing it. At first I thought it was just a malicious prank, but my curiosity was aroused, and I followed the man's suggestion. I came here to Riverton and learned the truth."

"And then the pay-off started."

"Yes. It's been all I could do to stay in school, the man took so much. He seemed to know exactly how much my allowance was."

"You've no idea who this party was?"

"Not the slightest. Always I had to leave the money in a different place. I was afraid to try to wait and see who got it—I'd been warned not to."

"Why did you pay off? Oh, I know you wanted to hush up the matter, but why was that so necessary?"

Mary Jorg looked at Henry Allen. She blushed. Henry said: "We've gone over that, Mr. Mort. Mary's in love with me, and she knows we could never be married if Dad found out or the thing became public."

"Did you know the same blackmailer was shaking down your mother, too?"

Mary Jorg started. Mort went on: "It seems to me that your wisest move would have been to go directly to your mother. Together you might have had some chance."

Mary Jorg stubbornly shook her head. "I'll never do that! It would break Mother's heart if she found out that I know."

"How many people have you told?"

"Why, Henry and Helen are the only two."

"You didn't tell Jerry Wales?"

"That little shyster? Why should I tell him, of all people?"

"I wondered myself. Did he have any way of finding out?"

"Of course not! I never saw him before this morning." She studied Mort. "What makes you think this man Wales knows?"

Mort shrugged. Helen Talbott appeared in the doorway. She seemed tremendously excited.

"That lawyer—Jerry Wales! He's been murdered! At Madam Malone's!" She eyed Mort confusedly. "The local newscast said you reported the murder to the police, Mr. Mort!"

Mort remained silent while everybody else seemed to speak at once. Allen wound up with: "You dirty double-crosser! You didn't tell us that Wales was murdered! You played me for a sucker, letting me talk. I knew you were acting city solicitor, but I didn't know about Wales. You should have told me any information I gave you would be used on the case!"

Mort eyed the youth calmly. "I gave you my word I wouldn't disclose Mary Jorg's identity."

"But you will try to track down Wales' murderer!"

"Of course. The assassination of lawyers is a practice I wish discouraged."

"Then the whole story will come out!" Allen turned wretchedly to Mary Jorg. "It's not my fault. You suggested that I hire Mort even when I argued that he couldn't be trusted. You kept saying he was the smartest lawyer in town—well, I hope you're convinced now!"

Mary Jorg eyed Mort coolly. "Do you think the police will accuse my mother of Wales' murder?"

"Her reputation won't help."

"So I thought. I fear for her. I wish you were working for her instead of against her."

"I am working for her."

"But how can you do that? You're the acting city solicitor. You're a paid public prosecuting attorney."

"But only for city ordinance offenses. There's no city ordinance against murder. It's a state offense. A city prosecuting attorney is free to handle a private practice even if it includes murder cases."

Allen looked bewildered. "But you said you were going to try to catch Wales' murderer!"

"Indeed I am. It so happens that I'm thoroughly convinced that Madam Malone is innocent. Catching the killer will be the quickest way to prove her innocence."

"Have you any idea who he is?"

Mort shrugged. "Oh, I know who the killer is." He appeared to be looking directly into Allen's eyes, but he was using the split-vision employed by basketball and tennis players. His gaze was neutrally focused on all three faces. Allen's expression was one of incredulity. Mary Jorg eyed him speculatively. Helen Talbott simply turned white. Mort smiled at her and walked wordlessly from the room.

THE PHONE was ringing when Mort entered his office. Mort answered. It was Ed Snyder, of the Mayhew Agency.

"You're a peach, you are!" Snyder exploded. "You hung up too soon. I've been trying to get you ever since."

"About what?"

"About this Talbott girl. I'm going to give you something off the record."

"Shoot."

"Some time ago Madam Malone hired us to nail a guy who was shaking her down. She didn't say what for. She didn't say anything except where the dough was to be picked up. So we staked out the spot for a day before the pay-off. It was a flop sub-division on the South Side, the Andover Heights. Maybe you've been down there. Only a half-dozen houses were ever put up, and even the street they're on is grown over with grass. The weeds were a couple of feet high on this street we cased. The only car that came down that way was a light green Packard. Guess who it belonged to?"

"The King of Belgium."

"No, it didn't. It belonged to this girl Talbott. What do you think of that?"

"What did you think?"

"That it was a blind lead. We checked on the girl and couldn't figure her with a blackmail racket. She's Society with a capital S, and the local credit bureaus give her an A-1 rating. So we figured her being out in Andover Heights that day was just one of those things."

"Why've you changed your mind?"

"I haven't. Only it's funny, your tying her up with the Wales job at Madam Malone's right away. That is, you gave us this Mary Jorg, and she led us straight to Helen Talbott. Who is this Jorg dame, anyway?"

"Oh, her old man's the King of Belgium."

Mort hung up and stared some seconds at the cradled phone. A key rattled in the door. Blackie Jones walked in.

"Well, what did you get?"

"Nothing. I went through everything in or on Jerry's desk before Chester got there. He was burned when he found me inside. You have to get up early in the morning to fool Chester."

"So you didn't find a thing."

"Nope. Unless maybe this means something." Blackie Jones reached into his inside coat pocket and withdrew a small red bank book. Mort accepted it, turned to the last page in which an entry was made. He whistled. He would never have believed that the little lawyer had died with fifteen hundred dollars in the bank. Nor would he have believed that Jerry would have been able to make deposits as large as two hundred dollars, the amount of the last three. Leafing through the book, he found that they tapered down to one hundred dollars, the amount of the first deposit, made a year before.

"You think it's something?" Blackie Jones asked hopefully.

"I'll say! It proves that Jerry was working for Madam Malone's blackmailer all along! The amounts represent ten per cent of the take. Jerry must have handled some minor part of the transaction, like making those phone calls."

"Whom do you think he was working for?"

"Your guess is as good as mine."

"I'll put my chips on Jack Chester."

"Did I hear my name mentioned?" asked a voice from the doorway. Chester walked grimly into the room. He eyed Blackie Jones sourly. "Listen, Blackie, if you didn't stand six feet-seven, I'd beat your ears off. You went through Jerry's desk. I want what you took out of it!"

Mort's brows lifted indignantly. "I resent your implication! What could my partner possibly have removed from Jerry's desk?"

"That little red bank book you're holding in your hand! Give it to me!"

"Do you think I'm crazy? Assuming that I do have any property of the late Jerry Wales, I'd be running a risk of a lawsuit to turn it over to anybody but his duly appointed administrator. The mere fact that you gave him desk space in your office didn't give you any right to his property."

Chester reddened. His face was inclined to be florid anyway, and he looked like a man on the verge of a stroke. "You can't kid me, C.D.! There's one man who has more right to that bank book than Jerry's administrator, and that's Garrett of Homicide! I'll see that he gets it!"

"Are you sure you want to do that?"

"Sure, I'm sure!"

Chester turned on his heel and strode from the room. Mort reached for the phone and dialed a number. When a voice answered, he said: "Good evening, Mr. Mayor. I've good news for you—I'm resigning as acting city solicitor. You can get another vote by appointing another boy. No, no reason for quitting except that I'm getting bored with it all. Thanks for the opportunity to serve, Mr. Mayor."

He hung up. Blackie Jones asked: "What was the idea of that?"

"I mean to keep the little red book. I can't conscientiously hold out on the city police so long as I'm a city official. My resignation put me in the clear."

"But Garrett—"

"Garrett can go jump in the lake. He can't prove the book is Jerry's. I'll let him have it when I'm ready. See who's fumbling around with the door."

The door opened as Blackie reached for the knob. Helen Talbott entered. She started when she beheld Blackie's bulk. Mort walked around his desk. "Greetings, Miss Talbott. By the way, is the night watchman on a vacation? He's supposed to call about visitors after hours."

"I didn't see any night man. The door was open and I—"

MORT SPRINTED for the light switch and actually had his hand on the button when the shooting started. An instant later the room was in darkness. Mort counted three more shots, all coming from the doorway. He saw a huge, crouching form move toward the door.

"Down, Blackie!" he snapped. "You're too big a target as it is. Miss Talbott, you lie flat on the floor!"

Orange flame flashed again from the doorway. Mort neither heard nor felt the slug, but he knew from the direction of the flame that it had come close. He flattened. Another burst of flame came from the doorway. It was the last shot. Mort waited five minutes and made Blackie wait the same period. Then he got up and turned on the lights.

"Is that wise?" Blackie demanded. "Let me look in the corridor. The guy may still be there."

"Not a chance. That gun-slinger's out of the building by now. But you can go and find the night man. It's ten-to-one somebody's put the slug on him and left him in a dark corner."

Blackie nodded, but first lent a hand to Helen Talbott. The girl got to her feet and smoothed her rumpled dress. She began to laugh.

"Go ahead," Mort encouraged her. "Some girls laugh when they're scared, others cry. I prefer the laughing kind." He nodded to Blackie, who left the room. In a few seconds the girl was normal again, though pale. Mort sighed.

"All right, tell me why you've come here."

"It's nothing important, really. Don't you think it can wait till you call the police?"

"The police will be here soon enough. And what you're here for is important. That bullet hole in the wall behind my desk tells that. It wasn't me the gun-wielder was after—it was you. Throwing a couple of shots at me was just for luck."

Helen Talbott became a shade paler. "Why, I can hardly believe that! I only wanted you to know that this lawyer who was murdered, Jerry Wales, could be the same man who's called up Mary demanding money of her. It never occurred to me that his voice was the same until after I found out he'd been murdered. It didn't register even then. I'd only talked to the man once—this morning when I paid him the five hundred dollars. Now I'm sure it was his voice on the phone."

"How many times did you hear it on the phone?"

"Twice. Both times Mary was visiting me."

"That's interesting. Now tell me, what were you doing in the Andover Heights section some weeks ago?"

Helen Talbott lost all color.

"How—how did you know that?"

"I asked you first."

"Asked what?" The voice was Garrett's. He walked into the room, flanked by his plain-clothesmen. His nose sniffed the air.

"Burned cordite! I smelled it in the corridor!"

"Not cordite," Mort corrected. "Just plain, American powder. Somebody emptied a revolver from the doorway. You may be able to find the slugs if you dig deep enough."

"Who was here at the time?"

"Miss Talbott, Blackie and myself. Miss Talbott is one of my clients. I think you'd better run along now, Miss Talbott. You've had enough excitement for one evening."

"Not so fast!" said Garrett. "Nobody leaves till I know what this is all about! Where's Blackie?"

"Looking for the night man. The odds are he got conked."

"Hmph! It's funny neither you nor a big lug like Blackie could nail the guy with the gun after he'd shot it empty."

"Some killers carry two guns."

"Well, this one must have been an amateur. I don't know how he could have emptied his gun at this range and missed every time."

"The light was out after the first shot, and it was hurried."

"Who was he after?"

"I wouldn't know."

Garrett scowled. "Look here, C.D., you can't get away with holding out on me. I've been thinking. As city solicitor you have to cooperate."

"I don't have to do anything. I've resigned. Ask the mayor."

Garrett made a move toward the phone, then checked himself.

"You know I can't be phoning up the mayor. I'll take your word for it. But it makes no difference. Solicitor or not, you can't hold out evidence. Let's have that bank book Chester told me about."

"Just where did Chester tell you about it?"

"He phoned Headquarters about ten minutes ago. Why?"

"He was in this building about ten minutes ago. He could have used a pay phone downstairs, then beat it back up here when he saw Miss—"

Mort stopped too late. He swore to himself for thinking aloud. Garrett jumped on the slip.

"So! The killer was trying to get this girl. I thought you told me she was just a client!" He whirled on Helen Talbott. "Come on, kid, let's have it—or do I have to drag you to Headquarters?"

The girl looked desperately to Mort.

"You're not dragging anybody anywhere," he told Garrett. "Get me Jack Chester, and I'll give you all the proof necessary to convict Jerry Wales' killer!"

Garrett started to argue, then checked himself.

"C.D., are you on the level?"

"Absolutely. Do as I say, and you can get all the credit for cracking the case."

"It's a deal. Where do you want me to bring Chester?"

"Madam Malone's."

Garrett's eyes widened. "You going to take this girl there?"

Mort nodded. When Garrett and his men had left, Mort turned to Helen Talbott and chuckled with satisfaction.

"At least I made him forget all about the bank book!"

"But I don't understand! You don't really expect me to go with you to Madam Malone's, do you?"

"I certainly do. It should be a unique experience for you."

Mort leafed through a phone book, found a number and dialed it. There was no answer. Blackie Jones came into the office as he put down the phone.

"You found the watchman?"

"Yes. He hadn't been tapped hard. I sent him to a doc, but only for the looks of it."

"Fine. We're all going to take a ride out to Madam Malone's." Mort turned to Helen Talbott. "Blackie's never been there. That'll make two of you."

Helen Talbott said: "Why do you insist on calling Mr. Jones 'Blackie'? He's fair and blond."

"His name's Blackstone after William Blackstone, the eighteenth century Oxford professor who first systematized common law. Blackie doesn't like such a long-winded name, so he shortened it."

Blackie scowled. "He should talk! He has kittens if anybody calls him by his full name, Clarence Darrow Mort. As if that's a name anybody should be ashamed of!"

Mort said gravely: "No, but I don't like to bear the name of somebody I resemble so slightly. I refer not only to physical appearance. The chief difference between Darrow and me is that while Darrow was the champion of the helpless, I'm the champion of the helpful."

Blackie shook his head. "That's not true, Miss Talbott. Mort's working right now not for fees but to bring justice to the killer of Jerry Wales! The fees he'll get are only incidental."

"That's a new name," said Mort, "for five thousand dollars!"

He picked up the phone again and dialed. Henry Allen answered this time.

"Sorry to drag you out again tonight," said Mort, "but I want you to pick up your fiancée and take her out to Madam Malone's. Yes, I said Madam Malone's. Well, suit yourself, only you're paying me to conceal her identity. I can't do that unless you do what I say. I mean it. Take her out there and nobody will ever know Madam Malone is her mother. That's better. We're meeting in the kitchen, so you can go in the back way. It's high time the girl went home!"

When he put down the phone, Blackie said: "Are you crazy? How can you crack this case without exposing the girl as Madam Malone's daughter? Especially if Madam Malone turns out to be the killer?"

"She won't. As for the other, leave it up to me. Let's get going."

THE MALONE kitchen was sufficiently large to accommodate all the guests, though there was a shortage of chairs. Madam Malone, worried, not daring to look at her daughter, remained standing. Mary Jorg also averted her gaze, as did Allen, who stood resolutely behind her. Garrett and his detectives occupied strategic positions. Jack Chester was plainly rankled. He glared at Mort, who stood calmly between Helen Talbott and his junior partner.

"Well," said Garrett, "it's your show!"

Mort's nod acknowledged his responsibility. "Jerry Wales was killed," he began, "because he was about to expose the name of a person who had been blackmailing Madam Malone. For this exposure he was to receive five thousand dollars. There was a delay in payment, and the blackmailer struck. He—"

"Just a minute," said Garrett, "What was he blackmailing Sadie about?"

"Sadie had a daughter," Mort explained, noting the sudden pallor in both mother and daughter. "The daughter is being educated among people who would shun her if her true identity were known."

Garrett eyed Madam Malone. "Is this true, Sadie? Where's the daughter and what's her name?"

"None of your damn business! C.D.'s my lawyer! He'll answer any questions." She said this a little doubtfully, her confidence in her lawyer apparently undermined. Henry Allen was looking daggers at the lawyer, who went blandly on.

"The blackmailer, of course, discovered that Jerry Wales was about to talk. So—"

"Wait a minute—how'd Jerry know the blackmailer's name?"

"Because Jerry was making all phone calls, giving all instructions as to where and when the money was to be paid. All this was done for a percentage. It was only ten per cent, but that was a lot of money for Jerry. You'll find all the entries here in this bank book, Garrett. You see, Jerry was putting all his ill-gotten gains aside as so much velvet."

Garrett accepted the book, leafed through it and frowned.

"Why the devil wouldn't you give me this before?"

"Because I didn't want you to have just enough facts to mess up the case. Nailing Jerry's killer is a matter of professional pride with me. He was a colleague, however undistinguished. So I wanted to save the evidence until I could use it with telling effect. I can do so now."

"I don't see," said Garrett, "how that proves anything against anybody but Jerry, and he's dead."

"It proves much more than Jerry's guilt. It proves the guilt of his accomplice, the real blackmailer. This young lady, Miss Talbott, told me earlier in the evening that Jerry was the man who called Sadie's daughter and demanded blackmail. But if poor old Jerry had been collecting from Sadie's daughter, his cut would have been banked along with his cut from blackmailing Sadie herself. So it follows that Jerry was not phoning the daughter to blackmail her and that Miss Talbott's statement to that effect is quite untrue."

Helen Talbott was on her feet.

"Why, you little liar! That was Jerry calling—I tell you it was!"

Mort smiled good-humoredly. "Calm yourself, Miss Talbott. My implication was not that you lied about Jerry's calls, only that your statement about them was untrue. You see, you have coupled first hand evidence with hearsay evidence. Your statement that Jerry did call is first hand and quite true. But your statement that Jerry called to demand blackmail is only hearsay, is it not?"

Helen Talbott looked puzzled. Mort pressed his advantage. "I thought so. Now who told you Jerry demanded blackmail?"

The girl hesitated. She eyed Mary Jorg, then said stolidly: "Mary did. Mary told me so."

"See, Garrett, it's as I thought. Jerry didn't call Miss Talbott's house to make blackmail threats—he called to make contacts with his principal—Mary Jorg! She's your blackmailer—and your killer!"

Sadie Malone said: "Oh, no! No, that can't be!"

"But it is," said Mort gently. "Mary Jorg knew all about your daughter—it was she who conceived the whole idea. Her own mother wasn't liberal enough in expense money at college, not from miserliness, but from motherly discretion. So Mary Jorg resorted to blackmail. Tell me, Sadie—when was it that you received the last demand for money?"

"A month ago. But another demand was due tonight."

"That checks. Today Mary Jorg paid Jerry five hundred dollars, thinking he could fix me so she wouldn't be sent to jail on a speeding charge. She begged the money from Miss Talbott, knowing her fiancé would make it good. She had to be free to collect the two thousand you were going to pay her. She—"

"That's not true!" Allen cried out. "Mary didn't have to blackmail anybody! I'd have given her all the money she wanted! She never asked me for a cent!"

"She was far too clever for that. She had to keep you off-guard, making a grandstand play of refusing help from you. She'd have had you hooked, my lad, but good!"

Mary Jorg said coolly: "You make circumstantial evidence sound very clever, Mr. Mort. But you can't convince a jury."

"Miss Talbott will. I don't think she's any longer willing to protect you for the sake of friendship. Especially since you tried to kill her tonight when you overheard from our conversation the fact that she'd been out to Andover Heights. Tell us, Miss Talbott, why you were out there."

Helen Talbott's eyes stared at the kitchen linoleum.

"I overheard the tail end of one of the conversations between Mary and Jerry Wales one day when I happened to pick up the phone extension. It didn't sound as if he were threatening her. She mentioned Andover Heights. I went out of idle curiosity."

"Idle curiosity that was almost your undoing. Mary Jorg jumped to the conclusion that you had overheard a lot more than that and tried to shoot you."

Mark Jorg was defiant. "Prove it!"

Jack Chester sighed deeply. "I think I can. I saw you go into the elevator while I was phoning Garrett."

"All right!" Mary Jorg leaped to her feet. A revolver materialized from her handbag. "Take it easy, everybody! I'm going out!"

Sadie Malone screamed: *"Mary!"*

The girl did not look at her. She moved back the detective on guard at the door, crossed the porch and disappeared. Garrett and his detectives had only taken a single step when the shot sounded.

"My God!" said Garrett, "maybe she's killed someone!"

"Only herself," said Mort. "Go get her, Garrett."

He ushered Sadie Malone into the next room.

"I'm sorry, Sadie. But give her credit, she shot herself because she knew a trial would reveal her identity. She couldn't let that happen—and bring disgrace on you!"

Sadie Malone turned back wearily to the kitchen.

"Thanks for trying, C.D. But that's my girl out there, and I'm claiming her. If only I'd have done it sooner!"

Mort watched her vanish beyond the door, then he reached into his pocket and withdrew the packet containing the five thousand dollars Sadie Malone had given him. He knew the money would mean nothing to her now, but he couldn't have taken money from her, even if she had offered him a coffin-full.